ANGELS OF CHAOS

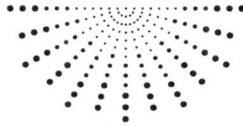

MAY DAWSON
ALEXA B. JAMES

Angels of Chaos

May Dawson and Alexa B. James

TABLE OF CONTENTS

CHAPTER ONE

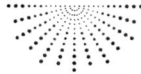

B rianna

"IF YOU WANT me to steal from the angels, you're going to have to stop cheaping out." I leaned back in my chair, facing down the man who wanted to hire me. "If they catch me…"

I ran my finger across my throat, then returned my hands demurely to my lap. I tried to look the part of the half-angel I was whenever I was out on the streets: long hair, sweet vintage dresses, flats for running from the police. Despite the occasional inconvenient *Wanted* poster, my sweetness-and-light act worked pretty well.

"No one ever catches you," he said. "That's why you're the best thief in Halftown."

Okay, it worked really well.

"Don't flatter me," I said, flashing him a smile. "I already know. What I don't know is if this deal is worth it for me."

"It's not about the money."

"I'm a thief, sweetheart It's always about the money."

"It's about what I want you to steal," he argued. "I heard you might have a special interest in Grace."

"Everyone has an interest in Grace," I said casually, but my heart began to beat faster.

The angels bartered some of their Grace—a renewable resource for them, as long as they only lost a little at a time—to rich and powerful humans. With enough money, anything was possible now that the angels had come to earth. With some Grace, a lost baby could be restored to life. Cancer could shrink until it vanished in a matter of seconds. The coma victim could open their eyes and smile.

Of course, people who couldn't be of service to the angels weren't worthy of their Grace. That's where I came in.

"Why would I work with you?" I asked, narrowing my eyes at the man across the desk.

"Because I can get you into the hospital in Paradise 12," he said. "You can walk in there like a runner for the Grace. But instead of it going to a rich asshole who isn't satisfied with ninety years of entitlement, it can come to me. And you."

I didn't trust his oily smile one bit. Grace was the kind of thing people killed for.

"Why me?" I asked. "Skip the part about how awesome I am. I love hearing it, but we both know there's something more going on here."

"Only an angel can walk through those doors," he said. "Or, perhaps, a particularly powerful Nephilim with unusually good luck."

I drummed my fingers absently against my leg. "You think I might not make it in."

"I'm sure you'll make it in, Crow. I'm not sure you'll make it *out*."

"Tell me more about how you're going to get me in there," I said. "Then I'll tell you if splitting the Grace fifty-fifty will be enough."

An hour later, I cut through what used to be an alley in Halftown. Now there were shanties made of metal and wood built between the brick walls. When the angels moved in, they took up nearly half of earth. That was bad enough, but the wars that came after had demolished even more of it. The city was still being slowly rebuilt, and as I made my way home along the narrow pathways through the rubble, I could see crumbling buildings against the skyline, stray dogs fighting over a cat carcass, and abandoned construction equipment. Hopefully, *temporarily* abandoned. We couldn't live like this forever. When the war moved on and left our city in shambles, the angels had promised we wouldn't have to live this way for long, that reconstruction would begin any day.

And yet, I knew if I went up to the roof of my building and looked to the north, I'd see the shining city of Paradise 12. They'd built their own cities while filling ours with rubble and empty promises. After all, an angel could never deign to live someplace like this. The rest of us? Yeah, we were on our own.

I wondered what asshole angel had sired me, but I didn't wonder very hard. That was the shit kids fought over. *I bet my daddy is Michael.*

I bet your daddy is a dickwad with wings, kid.

I was so lost in thought as I stepped from the makeshift road onto the street that I almost missed the Nephilim men that separated themselves from the rest of the trash.

"Brianna," said a teasing male voice. "No friends today?"

I turned as the three of them rose, carefully choosing their footing in the rubble as they spread out around me.

"No friends any day," one of them mocked me.

Adelphus, Remy, Marut. Marut was named for an angel, which always seemed especially humorous given his personality. Parents got uppity in Halftown, though. They wanted to believe their kids were better than the humans.

"Hey, school chums," I said. "So nice to see you again. It's been a while. Nice weather today, hmm?"

We'd known—but never liked—each other in the school where half-angels trained to be cannon fodder. Whatever godforsaken angel stuck his dick in my mom, I was born for the same reason as the rest. To fight the angels' war for them. They needed soldiers, and humans were too weak to fight demons—but not too weak to bear Nephilim children who could.

My mom had pretended it was for love before she died, but that was just what she had to tell herself. Angels didn't love anyone. They were a bunch of winged psychopaths.

Most of their progeny were psychos, too, though we didn't take flight.

We'd all graduated two years ago when we turned eighteen, but I couldn't seem to shake the neighborhood assholes. The three Nephilim were trying to circle me now. I rolled my eyes. "What do you want, Marut?"

His good eye narrowed. The effect was ruined because his other eye, the one that was scarred shut, couldn't narrow. He was trying to be scary, so I decided not to point out that he just looked lopsided. Harming the man's ego further wouldn't help move this conversation along.

"Depends. Can you replace what your ex-boyfriends took from me?"

"Ex-*boyfriends?*" I raised my eyebrows as I walked backward, carefully choosing my footing. "I think I'd remember that."

"Noah? Beckett? Rhyland? Ring any bells?"

The four of us had been inseparable for years. But that had all ended.

"Well, of course," I said, planting my hands on my hips. "*Other* school chums. I've been thinking about the reunion. We could do a disco ball, balloons, appetizers. Oh, and a DJ! What do you guys think?"

They rushed me.

Apparently they weren't party people.

I took one more step back, reaching down to wrench up the loose corrugated steel post that I'd sighted in the rubble when they approached me. As Marut reached me, I slammed it into the side of his head, and he crumpled to one side.

Adelphus was still coming in hot, and I flipped my new metal friend in the air so I could jab it into his belly. He let out a grunt of pain as he stumbled back. Remy grabbed me from behind, and I reached back, wrapped my arm around his neck, and with a heave, flipped him over my head. I planned to follow up, but he slammed hard into a pile of cinderblocks. I winced in sympathy. Unforgiving lands were a bitch.

Maybe I wasn't entirely sympathetic. I might be one of those non-winged psychopaths myself.

I rested the metal bar across my shoulders, wrists on top of it to brace it against my neck.

"We had the same training," I reminded them. "You boys really should have paid attention in class."

"You're just more powerful than any half should be," Adelphus groaned. "You don't deserve that power."

"None of us do," I reminded him. "Especially not our winged over-lords. But you get what you get, and you don't throw a fit."

Humming, I turned and headed for home.

CHAPTER TWO

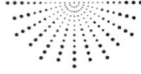

B*rianna*

"How was your day?" I asked, setting a bowl of thin soup in front of Gemma as she tugged her boots off. She closed her eyes for a second, as if fighting exhaustion at the thought of eating after a long day at work. I took the opportunity to study her delicate features, the dark circles like bruises under her eyes. I'd told those assholes who attacked me on the way home that all the Nephilim in Halftown had too much power, but it wasn't true. Gemma didn't have enough.

She opened her eyes and caught me watching her. "It was fine," she said, sounding more perky than she looked. "Long but uneventful. So... Good."

"Gemma," I said slowly. "Are you taking your meds?"

"Of course," she said, stirring her soup and avoiding my eyes. "You know I can't work without them."

"Are you taking the full dose?" I asked, sitting down across from her with my own bowl of watery soup.

"I'm taking enough," she said. "I'm working, aren't I?"

"You cut back," I said, narrowing my eyes at my best friend. My only friend, my conscience, my only confidant and comfort in Halftown anymore. We may not have been blood related, but she was the only family I had, and I sure as hell wasn't letting her skimp on her meds just because I hadn't pulled any good heists lately.

"I didn't want to run out before we had refilled it," she muttered into her bowl.

"Gemma," I scolded gently, taking her hand. "You can't do everything on your own. You should have told me you were running low."

I'd told that asshole this afternoon that I'd think about it—it was a dangerous job, and if I didn't make it out alive...

Well, Gemma may have been my only family, but I was more than that to her. Without me, she wouldn't survive. When her condition manifested in her early teens, her mother couldn't take care of her and left her to die. Like most Nephilim, she didn't know who her blessed angel father was, so he was no help. Which left me. I found her almost dead and snuck her home to nurse her back to health. Ever since, she'd been there for me every bit as much as I had for her. I wasn't about to stop now.

Which meant I had to take the job in Paradise 12. Fuck it. Wasn't like I had plans on Tuesday, anyway.

"I don't want you to worry about me, Brianna," Gemma said. "You have enough on your plate. And don't do anything dangerous."

I cracked a grin. "Me? Dangerous? Never."

"I mean it," she said, giving me a stern look. Gemma may have been born with one of the rare diseases that could affect Nephilim, one that sapped her of energy and left her so weak that without meds, she'd eventually lose even the strength to feed herself, but nothing could break her spirit.

"Wouldn't dream of it," I said, wiping my mouth with the back of my hand. I grinned wider, trying for an innocent look.

She rolled her eyes, letting me know I'd failed miserably. Me and *innocent* had parted ways long ago.

"If I cut the pills in half, I have enough to last until payday," she said, clearly not convinced by my act. Gemma was many things, but stupid was not one of them. "You know I'll be fine until then. I've done it before."

"Yeah, but you shouldn't have to," I said, grinding my teeth. "Your father is a fucking angel. You should be able to get Grace to heal."

"Brianna, I can't even fight demons like normal Nephilim, and you don't see angels healing all of them on the battlefield. Why would they make an exception for someone in an ammunition factory?"

Rage swelled inside me, and for the millionth time I wished I knew who her father was so I could hunt him down and punch him right in the pearly gates. But I didn't know, and my anger did nothing to help her. Not unless I used it to fuel my determination.

Which was exactly what I was going to do. I wished I could take her with me. If she could come along, even as a lookout, I knew she'd get as big a thrill from it as I did. But of course she couldn't come. That would have put her life in danger, too. Gemma was one of the strongest people I knew, tough and gritty as fuck, but without her meds, she couldn't survive, and even with them, she wouldn't be able to run if things went bad. She never complained about the hand she'd been dealt, and she worked harder than anyone I knew, determined to prove she was just as capable and worthy as the next guy. That's why I admired her as much as I loved her.

This heist would be for her. Even if she couldn't join me, she was my reason. This might be the most dangerous thing I'd ever done— scratch that, it definitely *was* the most dangerous—but after this, I could go back to petty crimes like I had before. After all, they wouldn't have hauled me in there if they didn't believe I could do it. They'd found me and made me a good offer because I was the best thief in Halftown. Hell, I was the best in the business anywhere. Period.

I squeezed Gemma's hand and got up, grabbing her bowl before she could insist on cleaning up since I'd cooked.

"Hey," she protested. "It's my turn to do dishes."

"Eh, you've been at work all day," I said. "I sat on my ass most of that time. You can get them another day."

8

When she didn't argue, my heart squeezed. I knew it was worse than she'd let on. That she was scraping bottom already. I didn't know if she'd make it until the heist, let alone her next paycheck. If I hadn't decided already, that did it. I was damn sure not going to let my friend waste away because the greedy angels couldn't be bothered to take care of their own. This was it. My big chance. Because this heist wasn't just going to get me enough money to buy Gemma's meds for a year.

It was going to get me enough Grace enough to heal her for good.

CHAPTER THREE

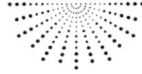

B*rianna*

ON TUESDAY NIGHT, I could hear Gemma tossing and turning even through the bathroom door that was too warped to close right. She must've been in pain again. My stomach knotted as I dressed, hoping the sliver of light seeping under the door wouldn't wake her.

No matter what happened to me, who I lost, how hard life got, I always came out on top. I had to trust that I would this time.

I could walk into the house of angels and walk out again at an easy pace with a smile on my face.

I glanced in the mirror, running my fingers through my long dark hair to give it more body. I'd dressed in the dark uniform of a full-blooded angel, the kind who had trained us. They'd always seemed conscious of their superiority as they walked the rows, watching us fight each other. I remembered meeting one's eyes as I lifted my bloodied face from the dirt, only to see the condescending way he looked down at me. Right before my opponent slammed his boot into my shoulder, knocking me down again, I'd seen the angel smile. He'd known what was coming.

I stared at myself in the mirror, subtly straightening my spine, lifting my chin, adopting the cold, arrogant persona I knew too well.

"It's the moment you've been training for all your life, Brianna," I told myself in the mirror. "Tonight, you get to be a bitch for a good cause."

I winked at my reflection and flicked the light switch before I opened the door. Then I moved through the apartment by memory, avoiding the creaky floorboards. I grabbed my backpack and slipped a plain trench coat over my shoulders to hide the uniform from anyone who knew me in Halftown. They knew damn well I was no angel.

I checked the pockets again to make sure they were empty save for my gloves, since I'd bought it to make sure nothing could be linked back to me. The costume was a death sentence if I were caught. The Warriors of Light didn't take kindly to being impersonated.

The hallway was pitch black, as was the city outside. Rolling black-outs had turned into *routine* blackouts, and tonight, that was fine by me. I made my way through Halftown to the rooftop of the building that stood closest to the high, shining wall around Paradise 12. Plenty of light on the angel side. Dropping my backpack to the ground, I pulled out my gear, checking the line connected to my robotic grappling hook before hooking it to the roof at my feet.

No guards on the street. I shed the trench and stepped onto the ledge surrounding the roof. Swinging the line connecting the grappling hook, I reminded myself of its weight. Then, I threw it toward the wall.

Bing-fucking-o.

It hit the top perfectly. The grappling hook's legs sank into the wall as it activated, and I breathed a sigh of relief. I'd pulled off step two of a complicated twenty-step plan. Now there were just a hundred other things that could go wrong.

I was ready for all of them.

I drew the line slack, then clipped my safety line carabiner in. I didn't plan to die tonight. At least not by my own hand.

I sat on the edge of the building, my feet dangling over the empty, broken street below. This was the hard part. I looked at the wall of Paradise 12, not down, as I reached out over nothing to take the line in both hands.

Then I pushed my feet against the brick wall and let myself fall.

My shoulders wrenched, but I didn't weigh much—angels were bird-boned to begin with, and food was expensive in Half-town. I kicked my legs up, catching my heels on the line. Then I pulled myself across the line until I reached the wall.

Straddling the wall, I paused for just a second. I had to get off the wall before someone saw me, but I spared one moment to look over Paradise 12. It always took my breath away. But up close like this... It was something else.

The angel's city looked like a garden broken by shining golden roofs and symmetrical pathways. Everywhere the angels went, they surrounded themselves with trees and flowers and luxury. The breeze carried the sweet scent of the blossoming trees below me instead of smoke and ash.

I pushed off the wall, landing in the soft grass below.

"Welcome home, Bri," I muttered, because no one would ever convince me that I didn't belong here as much as they did.

As if I owned the place, I headed toward the hospital, which was near gate four.

There was no rubble on this side of the wall. As I emerged from the park, I found myself surrounded by angels moving quickly about their business, even this late in the evening. They needed little sleep. Everything was perfectly orderly.

"Good evening, little sister," an angel greeted me warmly as he passed.

Instantly full of suspicion, I gave him a dark look. His eyes widened in surprise. Shit. Right. They were nice to their own kind, weren't they?

"Good evening, brother," I said, flashing him a smile, a second too late.

After that, I remembered to greet every angel I passed if they didn't manage to greet me first. The angels seemed to love to get a jump on *hello*. They were competitive bastards even when it came to being courteous.

The hospital was all white and gold and gleaming. If I woke up in this place, I'd assume the worst. You'd think waking up in Hell would be the worst, but I knew enough angels to know better.

I passed my forged papers over to the admin on the Grace floor. "I have an order from the governor."

The tall, red-haired angel looked me over skeptically, and my breath caught in my chest before she reached out for the order. But she groused, "What rich idiot are we wasting Grace on tonight?"

"The Grace is for an ill child," I said, which wasn't a lie, "lucky enough to belong to someone important." That part was.

The redhead snorted. "Maybe one day they'll let us decide who our Grace should be donated to."

"We could make our own deals," I said.

"I might like to give mine to someone who didn't already have every Grace rich humans can grant their children," she said before turning. "I'll be right back."

"Thank you." I flashed her a smile. Her words didn't fit what I knew of angels and their view of the world.

A few minutes later, she set a glowing ball in front of me. The Grace inside it moved and floated like a living thing; it seemed to shine, brightening the already-bright room. I forced myself not to stare, but when I dragged my gaze up to hers, she was watching me as if waiting for an answer.

"Pardon?" I asked.

"I just need your handprint," she said, pushing a flat black screen toward me. "To verify your identity."

"Of course," I said. I frowned down at the Grace. "It was supposed to be a double dose. She's dying."

"That's not what's on your paperwork," she said. "There is no other available donor tonight."

"Would you call my superior, please?" I asked, pointing to the number on the paper. "If this comes back wrong and the governor is displeased, I'd like to have done everything I can to straighten this out."

"Fine," she said, taking it from me. "Let me talk to my boss first and see if there's another dose available at the other hospital, just in case."

"Thanks so much."

As soon as she headed into the back, I palmed the Grace and slipped it into my bag, where it glowed through the fabric—fuck my life, I hadn't expected that—before striding toward the doors.

I was halfway down the hall when the alarms started blaring.

Now the fun begins.

I took off for the elevator, sliding under a gate when it started to slam shut. It echoed down the hall behind me, but I was one step closer to safety.

"Hey, lieutenant!" someone shouted.

Ha. Like I'd be on their side. I was starting to smile before I saw the guards in front of me.

I turned and dove through a hospital room, moving past a recovering warrior to the window. It was open, the gauzy curtains dancing in the fresh breeze.

"I never thought I'd see you again," the angel mumbled, as if in a dream. His eyes locked on me from a haggard face. There was something unsettling about an angel with no legs. The war took its toll on all of us, even them. "Come here, old friend."

"Rest," I said, already climbing into the window. "I'll see you another day. We'll talk more."

I leapt out the window, leaving the noise and chaos I'd created behind me, and sprinted down the long golden street, escaping their beautiful world.

CHAPTER FOUR

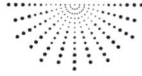

B *rianna*

M**Y FEET THUDDED** against the ground as I ran, ducking between buildings and angels out for their nightly strolls. I had no chance of blending in now, not while the hospital guards were hot on my tail.

The best thing would be to get the fuck out of Paradise 12 and back into Halftown. I could pull on my trench coat and disappear into the world of vagrants and other miscreants who would be out this time of night in Halftown.

Good luck finding me then, blessed fuckers.

Angels gaped at me as I ran past, their eyes filled with suspicion and concern as well as surprise. Apparently they weren't used to people making quick getaways. And why would they be? Angels had everything they needed right here in their little paradise on earth. It was outside the walls that things had gone to shit for the rest of us.

"Stop right there," yelled someone behind me. I dove behind a group of angels chatting outside a store and ducked into a side street.

I hoped their voices would cover my footfalls and buy me a couple seconds. And they did.

"Fuck yeah," I muttered, grabbing my grappling hook. I tossed it high, catching the edge of the wall and letting the prongs sink in. Behind me, I heard heavy boots hitting the ground.

But I was already gone. Ignoring their shouts, I scrambled up onto the wall of Paradise 12 and spared a glance down.

"You really don't want to go over there," shouted one of the men below. "It's not safe for our kind."

That made me chuckle. That sucker thought I was an angel. He thought I couldn't handle myself outside a literal paradise. Maybe he couldn't, but I was safer in Halftown than Paradise. I knew the dangers in Halftown—and exactly how to navigate them.

With a grin, I saluted the guards below, tossed my grappling hook to the roof I'd crossed from, and started across the wire. It wasn't like I actually had a choice. I couldn't stay in a Paradise. If I tried, I'd be discovered soon enough. And that wasn't an option, anyway. Not while Gemma was at home, wasting away from a disease the angels had brought. Not that they got diseases. They were perfect and all that shit. They only carried them, passed them on to weak humans. Or, you know, *blessed* us with them.

I was almost to safety when I heard the guards behind me. Fuck. I leapt to my feet on the roof in Halftown—I didn't miss the irony in my own thoughts, calling this place safety—and turned back. The two guards stood on the wall of Paradise 12, apparently arguing about whether to chase me further.

"Later, suckers," I muttered, grabbing my trench coat and taking off.

I heard a ripping sound behind me, and I glanced over my shoulder. The sight made my breath catch. One of the guards stood on the wall, tatters of his shirt fluttering down toward the ground far below. A pair of glorious white wings spread open on either side of him, each one stretching the length of his arms and beyond, at least as long as his entire, tall frame. He stood silhouetted against the lights in Paradise 12, which backlit his figure and edged his snowy wings in glimmering golden light. Even knowing the bastard would murder me when he found out I was a disposable Nephilim, I had to admit the sight was breathtaking.

Must be my weak human side.

I turned away and dashed down a dark alley in Halftown. Sure, angels were inhumanly gorgeous, but that didn't mean they were all goodwill and Grace. If they were, they never would have left Heaven in ruins and waltzed on down to earth, assuming humans would welcome them with open arms. Entitled shitheads.

A shadow passed over me, and I held back a despairing cry. There was no way I could outrun a winged angel while I was on foot, no matter how well I knew the streets of Halftown. I'd have to hide, and even with my trench coat, the ball of Grace was glowing through a bit, illuminating me. I turned a corner and ducked into the doorway of an abandoned building, almost losing my footing as my flats slid in the debris on the steps.

It wasn't perfect, but it was the best I'd be able to do for now. I'd have to come back for the Grace in the morning, when the angels had gone back to their precious paradise. In the meantime, I needed to lead them away from it.

I grabbed up some soggy cardboard, wrapped it around the globe, and reached through the busted window set in the door to drop it inside. I heard a masculine voice call out, and I was sure one of them knew where I'd gone. I had to get out of there—and fast.

Darting out of the doorway, I raced down the alleyway and onto the street. A rough-looking man in greasy jeans and a pair of steel-toed boots stood on the step of a boarded up building. He took a drag on his cigarette and gave me an appraising look as I passed, no doubt curious about my fancy clothes and wondering if I'd be easy prey. I had bigger concerns than a human looking for victims. Two much bigger concerns, to be exact.

Just as the man dropped his cigarette and stepped in my direction, one of the angels dropped to the road in front of me. I was moving way too fast to stop, and I slammed into him at full force.

Fuck!

17

It hurt like a bitch. Instead of tumbling to the ground under the force of the blow, the guy stood solid as a brick wall in front of me. Which meant I bounced off him like the soft human I was and fell flat on my ass at his feet. I scrambled up before he could move a muscle, looking for any piece of trash on the street that could serve as a weapon.

I grabbed an abandoned beer bottle, smashed the end off, and stood facing off with the angel, gripping a broken bottle. If I couldn't take him down, at least I could take an eye with me when I died. Or startle him and make a quick getaway while he was still reeling from the eye-gouging.

Like I said, I was as psycho as anyone else in Halftown. It was kinda a requirement to make it this far in life.

"She's not an angel," the angel growled, speaking to someone behind me, which I had to assume was the other guard. His voice sounded strangely familiar, but it was too dark in Halftown to make out anything but the outlines of his broad shoulders, tapered waist, and huge-ass wings.

"Nope," I said, brandishing the bottle and preparing to fight the good fight before they put me down like a rabid dog. That's what angels did when they caught people like me trespassing, conning them out of their Grace, and getting the jump on them as I escaped. Not that anyone else crazy enough to con the angels existed. That's why I'd been chosen.

I glanced behind me, and my breath caught. The second angel hovered in the air just above the street, floating like some beautiful, spectral ghost. His powerful wings stretched across the entire street, glimmering faintly in the darkness of Halftown.

Suddenly, the first angel struck. I spun back to face him, slashing with my bottle. It raked across his ribs, leaving a bloody gash. He barked some un-angelic words as he grabbed for me. I ducked, darting in to swipe at him again. But this time, he snatched the back of my neck and slammed me down on the pavement. My head hit the asphalt, and stars danced in my vision.

When I blinked the blackness away, I found him standing over me, his boot on my chest. I struggled, but I was no match for a full-blooded angel.

"Tell me where the Grace is, and I'll make it quick," he said, pulling a knife from his belt.

"Bless my ass," I said, spitting the words at him.

"Believe me when I tell you that you really want me to make it quick," he said, his eyes cold as he leaned down over me.

That was when I really got a good look at him, up close and personal. And even though it was dark, the familiarity of his features made my blood run cold.

Fuck. I didn't just know his voice. I knew *him*. Well, I had once upon a time, anyway. But I guess, really, I'd never known him at all. I'd sure as shit never known he was a full-blood.

Noah.

His eyes narrowed, and I saw the moment it clicked into place for him, too.

"Actually," he said slowly, a cruel smirk twisting his perfect lips. "I think this one needs to be taken into custody until she's ready to talk."

CHAPTER FIVE

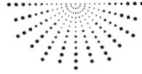

B*rianna*

I DIDN'T EXPECT to be dragged back into Paradise 12, although this time, I walked through the Pearly Gates.

Well. *Walked* implies a level of dignity that was not happening. My hands were cuffed behind me, and Noah wrapped his hand around the nape of my neck, pushing me forward ahead of him. The sensation of his fingers on my neck, controlling, domineering, reminded me of the past in a way that made me want to knock his teeth out. He'd ghosted me after our last heist together, and I'd never seen him again. And now I knew why. He was a fucking angel.

I hated having his hands on me, hated the effect he had even more. Because despite everything, despite time passing and accepting that he was never coming back, the wound was fresh all over again now that I'd seen him. Not only that, but the betrayal of knowing he'd never been who he said he was, that he hadn't been a Nephilim who was caught and died that night, but that he'd been a calculating angel who'd walked away voluntarily and lived in a literal paradise all these years while I barely kept myself and Gemma alive eating onion soup, hurt worse than it should. The fact that I hadn't known made me hate not just him but myself. I'd given myself to a man who had been lying through his teeth all along, about everything down to his very identity, twisted like a knife in my back. I'd fucking loved him.

"Why the fuck are you touching me?" I demanded, trying to jerk free of him.

"Watch your mouth." Noah's lips dipped close to my ear, bringing him close enough to me to send a shudder up my spine. Whether it was fear or desire or a disturbing mix of both, I couldn't tell. "Show a little respect for once."

"I don't have any respect for you."

His fingers tightened at the base of my neck, his blunt fingernails digging into my skin. "I can teach you some," he warned me, his voice dark.

"You used to be such a nice boy," I taunted. "What happened?"

He snorted. "And you're still a liar."

We entered one of the beautiful buildings—they all looked alike to me—and Noah marched me through a glittering marble lobby to an interrogation room. Funny, but an interrogation room had the same furniture and air of hopelessness no matter where you were.

"Why do you have interrogation rooms in Paradise?" I demanded, whirling to face him as he closed the door behind us, leaving the other angel outside. "You're all perfect. What is there to question?"

One corner of his mouth tugged up in a familiar way. It sent a twinge through my heart before I glanced away. That smile almost made me expect something else from him than dickish angel behavior, even though I knew better now. I knew what he was, even if it was just now sinking in. He'd never been my boyfriend, my lover. He'd always been a monster.

"You think I'm perfect."

"Oh, Jesus. This is embarrassing. Please tell me you didn't arrest me so you can flirt with your ex."

"Sit." He looked meaningfully at the chair on one side of the table.

He held all the cards at the moment—except that I was the only one who knew where the Grace was—so I sat and offered him my largest, sunniest smile.

"You should be grateful to be arrested," he said. "I could have killed you, and no one would have blinked an eye."

"Oh, gee, thanks," I said, rolling my eyes. "My bad. I'm ever so grateful, your majesticness."

"Enough with the sarcasm," he growled.

"Aren't you supposed to be the good guys? Boasting about how no one gives a fuck if you murder people doesn't make you sound very nice, Noah."

"No one thinks we're nice. They think we're their saviors."

"Shows how fucking desperate humanity is," I muttered, slumping back in my chair.

He stared at me long enough to be disconcerting. His eyes were eerily bright. "Do you ever make it through a sentence without cursing?"

"Not often," I said with a smirk. "I seem to remember you having a varied and profane vocabulary. But now you're doing the full-blood whatever-this-is, huh?" I had to nod at him instead of gesturing because my hands were still restrained behind my back. "Want to take the cuffs off?"

He glowered at me. "No."

"I thought you'd leave me in an interrogation room to cool down." That was what I wanted. Some time to catch my breath and plot my next move. Being caught and almost being killed was bad enough. Facing down my one and only ex? That was a real mindfuck.

"If I ever need amateur psychology tips on how to do my job, I'll be sure to consult you," he said. "Now, where'd you hide the Grace?"

"Does it matter?" I asked. "You're going to kill me anyway."

He shook his head. "No, I'm not."

"How come when you say that, I don't even think it's good news? I assume there's a terrible fucking punchline?"

"There you go again," he said. "That wasn't even necessary. It's embarrassing."

"Stop critiquing my language and tell me what you're really up to. You wouldn't go to all this trouble for just the Grace." God in Heaven —not that He was anymore—Noah still drove me crazy. The calculating son of a bitch had some kind of scheme, I could tell. I just didn't know what it was.

"Seeing you restrained is really no trouble at all," he said. "Where's the Grace, Brianna?"

"I dropped it when I was running away. If your people didn't manage to find it, then they're either idiots or someone else got to it first, and they're also idiots."

"You never drop something you've gone to all the trouble to steal."

Fuck. He still knew me as well as I knew him.

He smirked like he knew he'd got me. "Oh, Brianna. Don't you want me to just walk you back to the gate and let you go?"

I stared at him, at that sensuous mouth about the jaw that could cut glass.

Of course I wanted that, but it was not on the list of options. Noah seemed determined to break me with a ferocity that was complimentary, really. I had dug under his skin.

The fact that he was a gorgeous splinter lodged under *my* skin was irrelevant.

"I don't have the Grace," I said. "I can't tell you where to find it now. This whole conversation is pointless."

It was an especially pointless conversation for me. They weren't going to let me go. I'd strolled into a hospital in Paradise 12—someplace my kind weren't even allowed without an escort and a favor— and walked out with their most precious commodity. I wasn't even going to prison. This story would die with me before I inspired others to the pinnacles of human stupidity.

Noah had been prowling around the room, but he stopped behind me. He grabbed the back of my chair as he leaned down and growled into my ear, "Why won't you let me help you?"

Surprised laughter burst from me. "Because I know you aren't going to?"

"You're even stupider than I realized," he said, his fingers tightening against the back of my chair as if he wanted to hurt something. Or *someone*. "And I thought you were quite foolish."

"Right back at you, dickweed."

The way he talked now was strange. He'd growled that *stupid* the same way he would have years ago. He'd called me *quite foolish* in a far more posh tone. He should really pick a persona and stick with it.

"What'd you steal it for?" he snapped, shoving off the chair.

"Money." There was no point in denying my guilt.

"Who'd you steal it for?"

"Come on. I'm not telling you that."

He barked out a laugh. "Oh, now you're not a traitor?"

"I was never a traitor." The fact that he thought that got under my skin in a way none of his other comments had. "But seeing as how you're an angel, I can't say the same about you."

"I'm not the traitor." He stopped his pacing to caress the back of my neck, and then his fingers teased up the knobs of my spine until they slipped into my hair. He twined his fingers through the strands, winding it around his fingers.

Then he snapped my head back, arching my neck. I met his glittering eyes, blinking to keep my eyes from watering with the sudden pain. He used to do that move in sexy way. Now it was just painful.

"Oh yeah?" I said, managing to laugh. "Then what do you call it when you pretend to be on someone's side when really you're the enemy?"

He ground his teeth together, glaring at me without speaking, though I could see the fury inside him. I'd dared to call him out, after all.

"Come on, Noah, tell me what you really think of me. Unleash that dirty mouth. The real you. You're an asshole either way, but I liked the old you better."

He released me suddenly, like I disgusted him. "Tell me where the Grace is, and I'll let you walk out of here."

"Oh? How many steps past the gate before you gut me and leave me in a gutter? A knife in the back must be a specialty of yours. How did I never see it?"

"I wouldn't leave you in the gutter. Not right in front of the gates." He managed to sound scandalized as he mocked me.

"Fuck off," I said. "I'm not telling you anything."

"Then you're going to prison," he said. "Nothing I can do about that."

"Really? You're not going to kill me? How kind of you."

His circuit of the room was almost complete, his every movement smooth and predatorial, so I could see the flicker of a smile on his lips when he turned to me.

"Oh, sweetheart," he said. "I'm not doing you any favors. Trust me."

"Why don't you just kill me?"

"I've got bigger plans for you than the easy way out, baby girl."

Prison. But it was more than that. There was a reason we never heard stories about the angel prisons. Because no one ever lived to tell. But there were rumors.

Noah knew I'd stolen from his kind, and he was going to find a way to get the truth out of me… And he wanted to be paid in more than blood and death.

The way I lived, I'd always known I was going to die young and bloody. I'd been raised for the war, for fuck's sake. I'd made my peace with a precarious future. But this was someone else's plan, one where I couldn't see what was coming. I just knew there would be pain and torture.

Fear, deeper and darker than the fear of having my throat slit, wormed its way through my belly.

"You're a monster," I whispered, fear curling through my voice no matter how low it was.

He leaned across the table, resting his knuckles on the wood. I glared up at him.

His voice was soft when he said, "I guess you'd know. *You* made me one."

25

CHAPTER SIX

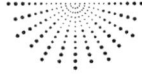

N^{oah}

I NEEDED A DRINK. Better yet, five or six. As I watched the surveillance footage, I could see Brianna taking the Grace and waltzing right out of the hospital. She'd always had balls.

"What do you think?" Cael asked, watching over my shoulder. He'd been with me when we took Brianna in, and he'd kept his mouth shut when my behavior was definitely not my usual. I liked the man all the more for it.

I thought a whole shitload of things, but most of them weren't fit to be repeated here.

"I'll find out where she stashed it," I said, crossing my arms and turning to the camera that showed her now, sitting in her holding cell waiting to be shown to her permanent home if she didn't cooperate.

"O-kay," Cael said.

The bastard sounded doubtful.

So, this was how the ghosts of my past were going to catch up to me. Brianna didn't know it, but she'd done a lot more than betray me. She'd distracted me. I'd had one job—to find the demonspawn hidden among the Nephilim. That had been my assignment when I was just a ten-year-old kid, sent off to one Halftown's hellish Nephilim military academy. I'd been so eager to prove to the elder angels that I was worth something.

And then I'd met Rhyland and Beckett, and we'd become fast friends. Later on, Brianna had overheard Rhyland making snide comments about Gemma's weakness, and she'd decided that pummeling him was the most effective way to get an apology.

Beckett had just watched, the little psycho. So, I'd taken it upon myself to break up the fight. I'd made them kiss and make up, and from that moment on, we'd had respect for Brianna's fighting abilities —and her temper.

I'd never expected to get sidetracked by the Nephilim. I'd never expected to become a part of their gang, to get so caught up in their schemes that the next thing I knew, I was stealing from my own people. I told myself—and the elders—it was a good cover. If I went along, the Nephilim would never suspect me. They'd trust me, help me flush out the demonspawn among them.

The thefts weren't even for Brianna. That girl never wanted a thing for herself. But in a way, it was for her. At least, I'd done my part of it was for her. She might have done it for Gemma, but for me, it was always for Brianna.

I'd left that weakness behind me, though.

And now here she was, the girl who'd created so much havoc. The girl who had somehow slipped away, disappeared without a trace, and left the twins and me behind, in all kinds of trouble.

Brianna stood and paced the tiny cell. She could barely do more than turn in circles. She jiggled the door handle, then bent to examine it. The little sneak was probably checking to see if she knew how to pick the lock. But the locks here were nothing she'd seen in Halftown —and nothing anyone could pick. I smirked at the screen, a ridiculous sense of pride swelling inside me. Pride that I shouldn't feel about an ex-girlfriend who had, in the end, chosen herself over me.

And I didn't give a single fuck about that.

I left the office and returned to her cell, knowing she wouldn't talk but hoping against my better judgment that she would. I just had to find the thing she cared about enough to make her talk. And I knew just what that was. The only person who had ever mattered more to Brianna than herself.

Gemma.

I stepped into the holding cell, forcing Brianna to step back against the wall if she didn't want to be standing toe to toe with me, practically in my arms. My cock jerked at the thought.

Fuck.

I was not going to think that way about this sexy little traitor. I'd fallen for that shit before. I was older and wiser now.

"I know why you stole the Grace," I said.

"I don't know what you're talking about," Brianna said, crossing her arms over her chest and glaring up at me.

I still didn't get it. I had turned over that heist-gone-wrong a hundred times, and I'd never figured out how she could have killed an angel. Nephilim weren't strong enough to take down an angel on their own. So, who had been with her? My money was on the twins, though those little shits would never admit it. They swore they'd stuck to the plan. But even three Nephilim weren't supposed to be able to take down an angel.

Unless we'd over-hyped ourselves.

"It had to be for Gemma," I said, a note of challenge entering my voice. "Wasn't it? That's what you were stealing for last time."

She scoffed. "What, you've been watching me for three years? How do you know what I did last time?"

"You know that's not what I mean," I gritted out.

"Oh, so you're referring to the last time I saw you, when you and the twins disappeared on me and left me to escape the patrols *by myself*, dragging a nearly unconscious Gemma along with me?"

"Why didn't you get her medicine?" I challenged. "She should have been plenty healthy by the time you disappeared from our old neighborhood."

Brianna's eyes narrowed. "How do you know when I left?"

"You didn't think we'd let you take a heavenly relic and walk away with it, did you?" I asked.

"So, you ratted me out to your big, powerful angel friends, and you all came looking for me, but I wasn't there," she said.

It was close enough to the truth, which pissed me off. But I wasn't going to let her know she'd gotten to me. "You stole from the angels," I said with a shrug, as if that explained everything.

Brianna rocked back on her heels, still studying me. "You know what I'll never understand? I can't figure out why an angel would want to live in a shithole Halftown. Go to our school. You could've been here. Or are you so sadistic you just did it to fuck with us for fun?"

I had my reasons—my orders—but I wasn't about to go into it with her.

"If you're not going to tell me what you did with the Grace, allow me to show you to your new home," I said, giving her my most fiendish smile. No way was I telling this girl more than she'd already figured out on her own. Which was too much.

"Fine," she said. "Take me."

I didn't hesitate. I was going to enjoy watching this place destroy her. Just like she'd destroyed me.

In that one night, that one heist gone wrong, she'd taken more than some old relics. She'd blown my cover, thereby making me lose my prestigious position hunting down demon-spawn. She'd also cost me the respect of the angels I'd taken the assignment to impress in the first place. On top of that, she'd ensured my friends—our friends— never spoke to me again without boiling hatred in their eyes. She'd taken everything I'd worked for all those years.

And now, I was going to take just as much from her.

CHAPTER SEVEN

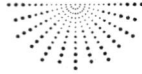

B *rianna*

THE REALITY of where I was headed only truly sank in as the heavy iron door slid into the wall with a clang of finality. I swallowed hard at the echoing sound of the prison beyond. Noah gripped my upper arm tighter, hustling me through the door and along a corridor with barred cells on either side. Each cell held two metal bunk beds against the back wall, a toilet, and zero privacy. The other prisoners stared out at me, their looks ranging from curious to predatory, wary to malicious.

"Dead Nephilim walking," I muttered to myself.

"You won't be that lucky, sweetheart. You won't die until I'm through with you." Noah's voice in my ear was too close, and I shivered. When had he turned into such a fucking creep? Oh, yeah, he'd always been one. I just hadn't known.

Our footsteps echoed through the chamber, which looked about the size of a large gymnasium. Above our walkway was a second one, with cells opening off it as well. I quickly did the calculations in my head, trying to estimate how many other half-humans were here with me.

I'd always figured the angels killed most criminals, considering them disposable, but maybe I'd been too quick to jump to that conclusion. I'd guess there were at least 200 bunks in this prison alone, and though I was pretty sure it was the only one in Paradise 12, that seemed like a high number. Which had me wondering what evil they had planned for me and the other prisoners.

"Right in here," Noah said, jerking me to a stop outside one of the cells. "Until you're ready to talk."

"Never gonna happen," I reminded him, trying to sound less concerned than I felt.

"Then you can rot in there with the rest of them," Noah said, opening a cell and shoving me inside a cell.

Them.

When I'd known Noah, he'd been one of us—or so I'd thought. He'd grown up in Halftown with me and the boys, and I'd never had any reason to suspect he was an angel. Why had he hidden that? I mean, there was the obvious reason. We all hated the angels and would have turned on him. But that was beside the point. He would have had all the power. He didn't need us to be his crew. He could have been in one of the paradises, having a crew of pureblood angels blowing sunshine up his ass and singing his praises, or whatever the fuck angels did in their schools. Why had he hidden in Halftown pretending to be a Nephilim all those year?

I wasn't about to ask him that now, to act like I cared. I shouldn't care. I *didn't* care.

I ignored the tightening in my chest that said otherwise.

Caring was a weakness. I was well aware of that fact after being Noah's girlfriend. He obviously hadn't given a shit, and look where he'd ended up. I'd cared, and look where I'd ended up. That was all the proof I needed—not that I needed any. I'd known that for the past several years, since I'd left the academy, and my friends had disappeared without a word of goodbye. Well, fuck them, too. Now it was just me and Gemma, and that was just the way I liked it.

Shit.

I had to get back to Gemma.

I turned to say something to Noah, but he'd already slid the bars closed between us. I stared out at him, and he stared in at me, and neither of us spoke for a second. That stupid fluttery feeling started in my belly again. Noah chose that moment to turn and stalk off without another word, punctuating my assessment of my own body's responses to him. *Stupid.*

"Well, if it ain't the new girl," drawled a voice behind me. I spun back to the three girls sitting on the bunks behind me. I scanned them in one glance, trying to peg them as friendly or hostile. But their faces weren't giving anything away. The one who'd spoken had light brown skin, her sleek black haired pulled up in a ponytail so tight it must have hurt, and her eyebrows clearly drawn on with a pencil. This gave me hope. If a girl could get makeup in here, surely one could get a message out.

"That's me," I said, trying not to sound either meek or aggressive. I didn't need enemies.

I didn't need friends, either, though. I wasn't planning on sticking around long enough to need them. It was a rule I'd made for myself when the last batch turned traitor and disappeared on me, leaving me to care for Gemma on my own.

"What you in here for?" asked the girl on the bunk above the first one. She had a shock of lemon-yellow hair on one half of her head while the other was buzzed so close I could see her pale skin through it.

"I refused to talk," I said, nodding my head back to where Noah had disappeared. They'd heard him confirm as much.

"That's good," said the third girl, who was sitting on the other top bunk. "The worst thing to be in this place is a rat." She was so small I wasn't sure if she was an adult or if they threw kids in this place, too. She had dark brown skin and a buzz cut dyed the same lemon-yellow as the other girl. That made me think they'd maybe dyed their hair together, and if a girl could get hair dye in this place…

"I don't plan to stay long, but I might as well introduce myself," I said. "I'm Brianna."

That drew a snort from the first girl who spoke. "That's what they all say. And I'm Anna."

"Erelah," said the second girl.

"Samarah," said the third girl.

"Cool," I said. "So. Who would I talk to if I needed to send a message to someone in Halftown?"

"You don't have anything on you to trade, do you?" Anna asked, looking me up and down. "Because the price is high in here. Nothing's free, baby. We'll want our pound of flesh."

I shrugged. "I know. I just want to know for when I have something."

Anna slunk down off her bed, moving like her bones were made of liquid. She stepped closer to me, her eyes narrowed and glinting. I automatically took a step back, only to press up against the bars of the cell. "Then I'm the one you want to talk to," she said, her right hand balling into a tight fist. "But first, tell me what you're going to give me for it."

I wasn't about this bitch pushing me around from the start. I knew how I responded to these girls would follow me every day that I was here. I wasn't planning on that being many, but first impressions counted. What I did now gave me a reputation. It either told other girls they could fuck with me, or it told them I was best left alone.

I was never one to go down without a fight.

"Touch me, and I'll give you a fist right in your face," I said as the other two flanked Anna, all three of them looking at me like a shiny new punching bag they couldn't wait to break in.

"Pat her down," Anna said, and Erelah leapt forward, her yellow hair flopping to one side. Before she could touch me, I grabbed a handful of it and spun her around, slamming her down on the cement floor on her back.

The second she hit the floor, the entire cell block came to life. I'd been so busy talking to the girls that I hadn't noticed anyone else. But they must have been noticing me, because what sounded like a hundred people started banging on the bars of their cells in unison, the metallic clang echoing through the huge hall. A hundred voices chanted in rhythm with the banging, a chorus familiar to everyone who's ever gone to school—"Fight! Fight! Fight!"

"I guess you didn't hear me," Anna said. "I run shit around here."

"Come at me, bitch," I said, bouncing on my toes, my fists at the ready. I'd taken down plenty of assholes in my life, and I wasn't about to start cowering now.

"Who you calling a bitch?" she asked, her lips drawing back from her teeth in a snarl.

"Whoever fits the description," I said, glaring back at her.

She threw a punch, but I ducked and hammered my fist into her side. She crumpled in half, falling to her knees. I didn't have time to finish her off before Samarah leapt at me. She grabbed a handful of my hair and threw all her weight into it. I crashed to the floor, hooking my leg behind hers as I fell to bring her down with me.

Before I could scramble around and straddle her, someone grabbed me from behind. I was hauled off the struggling girl and slammed against the bars. A strong arm reached through, pinning me against them. My nostrils filled with a heady, familiar scent. God, I still remembered the way he smelled. Too damn good.

Muttered curses met my ears as a key jingled against the bars, and then the door swung open. Noah hauled me out and slammed the door just as Anna leapt up and smashed into them from within. Noah released me, dropping me to the floor as he locked the cell.

I heard a laugh that sent a shiver straight down my spine. I knew that laugh. It was chillingly familiar. My heart stopped beating, and the world fell away. I couldn't hear the banging and the chanting. I couldn't hear anything but the echo of that unhinged, hyena laughter as I lifted my eyes to the cell three down from mine, already knowing who I'd find behind the bars.

CHAPTER EIGHT

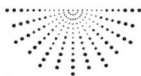

B*rianna*

"YOU CAN'T STAY out of trouble for ten minutes, can you?" Noah said as he grabbed my bicep and dragged me up. I scrambled to my feet, wanting to jerk away from him, but his fingers tightened around my arm.

Adrenaline coursed through my body at the thought of being locked up with my former nearest and dearest. Before I could swing at Noah, he grabbed my wrist with his other hand, his fingers bruisingly tight. His lips brushed against my ear as he stepped close to me, the heat of his body washing over me.

"I don't want to have to hurt you," he murmured in my ear. "And if you hit me in front of all these prisoners, baby girl, I'm going to have to hurt you."

If he didn't want to hurt me, I wouldn't be in prison, would I? But I didn't doubt his threat. I stilled, keenly aware of his body against mine, and not wanting to rub up against him by struggling.

"We'll see you later," Anna promised me as Noah strode forward, his hands propelling me back. I reluctantly took a step backward, then another, hating that I couldn't see where I was going but powerless to stop him.

I locked eyes with Anna over Noah's shoulder. "Can't wait."

Noah's lips quirked, as if he were laughing at me. "Since you can't seem to make new friends," he said, "I guess you should stick with old ones."

He spun me around, his fingers grabbing my shoulders, and I came face-to-face with a familiar face through the bars.

Rhyland, my favorite little psycho.

The chaos twins had identical gorgeous faces, but one was a dark-haired asshole Nephilim and the other was a blond-haired asshole Nephilim. It was the blond one I faced now. He was grinning, clearly delighted that Noah was threatening my life instead of protecting it.

"Look at that, the gang's all back together," Rhyland drawled. He leaned his shoulder against the bars, his arm crossed over his chest. "And everyone who meets Bri still hates her."

"Hate's a strong word," I said. "But if we're talking about our feelings now, this one's mutual."

"Fucking bitch!" Anna called down the cell block, rattling the door of her cell. "I'm going to turn your intestines into shoelaces!"

"That doesn't even make sense," I muttered, shaking my head.

"Get him out," Noah called to someone down the hall, jerking his jaw toward the door next to Rhyland's. "I'm taking this cell for her."

"Right next to him?" I asked, arching a brow as a guard opened the cell door. "You better be ready to find a very dead guy in that cell tomorrow morning. I'm not too fond of any of you assholes anymore."

"A little gratitude would be nice," Noah growled. "I could put you in with him, if you'd like that better." His lips scraped the shell of my ear, and I jerked away.

"Stop fucking touching me, you piece of shit. And I'd be happy if you put him in the same cell with me. It'd make it a hell of a lot harder for him to run from me like he did last time."

"Don't tempt me," he said. "Until you start talking, you don't get to ask for anything."

"I wasn't asking. I was responding to your threat. And you're never going to get what you want from me. I'm no traitor."

"Funny, because none of us would be here if you weren't."

I twisted to face him, or tried to, but his hand wrapped around the nape of my neck, forcing me to keep looking forward. What the hell did he keep going on about, calling *me* a traitor? When things went south for us all, I was the one who ended up left behind in Halftown. They all ran.

The Nephilim who was being evicted from his cell was apparently attached to it. He put up a fight, but was dragged out, bloody and glaring.

His eyes locked with mine. "I'm going to fucking kill you, little girl."

Great. More friends.

I flashed him a smile. "Fantastic. Sounds like a plan. It'd be better than listening to Rhyland prattle on."

"You still talk a lot when you're terrified, don't you?" Rhyland asked, watching me with his eerily pale eyes.

"Oh, so you must be the crazy one," I said as Noah pushed me into the cell. "I'm not scared of you." I stumbled with the force of the shove, but I caught myself in the center of the room and made myself turn, looking relaxed.

"You should be," Rhyland said. His once playful eyes held only hatred for me now.

"Think about my offer, baby girl," Noah promised me as he banged the door shut between us.

"It wasn't much of an offer," I pointed out. "And I'm not your *baby girl*."

"You'll answer to whatever I want to call you."

I snorted out loud, choking on my laughter. "Keep dreaming, angel scum."

He touched his finger to his forehead in a mocking salute. "Good luck. I'll see you tomorrow."

At least for tonight, I was safe in my own cell, separated from all my new friends. The last owner of this particular cell had been moved across the walkway, but he was still yelling at me. I forced myself not to watch Noah stride down the walkway. He was an asshole who literally wanted to murder me and dance on my grave, and yet part of me felt a weird sense of longing when he left me.

But fuck all that. I was *always* alone. Shouldn't bother me now.

I crossed my arms over my chest and studied the cell around me, doing my best to ignore Rhyland, even though I could feel his gaze on me. Tension whispered across the back of my neck, even with the bars between us.

The previous occupant had left behind crumpled blankets on a still-warm mattress. I crinkled my nose, moving instead toward the bunk on the other side—as far from the asshole twin as I could get. I might have been talking shit to Noah, but I was tempted by the thought of strangling Rhyland nonetheless.

"Where's your evil twin?" I asked. Though Rhyland just pissed me off, I dreaded seeing Beckett. If Rhyland thought I was a traitor, so would his brother, and Beckett wasn't exactly the forgiving type.

"Solitary," Rhyland said with a crooked grin that revealed a missing molar.

"What did he do?"

"He hurt someone."

"Beckett always had a knack for that," I said lightly.

I tucked my raven hair behind my ears and turned, crossing my arms over my chest. Rhyland was still grinning, as if the sight of me behind bars made him happy. That made two of us.

"What did you do?" Rhyland asked me.

I chewed my lower lip, running my fingers through my hair. I shouldn't talk to him, and yet I still felt so jumpy, it was hard to ignore him like I should. I shook my head, regretting having started the conversation at all.

Think about the last time you saw him.

Rhyland and Beckett and Noah never showed at our rendezvous point after everything went to hell. I'd waited for them as long as I

38

dared, then slipped out to get Gemma. Everything was fucked and I knew we had to lay low. I'd been able to hear angels swooping overheard intermittently; they were so silent until they were right on top of you. I'd been so sure the others would show up. I knew they'd gotten away. I'd seen them escape, and I'd run, too. But I'd returned every day, confusion and hurt tearing at my heart like the wild dogs that ran the streets of Halftown. I was sure they'd come back for us, take us to whatever Halftown they'd found a new home in. But they'd never come back for us, never even left a note.

Eventually I'd accepted the reality: they'd left me to care for Gemma on my own. She was the only person who hadn't turned on me, who had stuck with me when things were at their worst. Which was why I had to get out of here and find my way back to her.

Seeing them here… They must have kept doing heists, like I had. And like me, they'd gotten caught. I shouldn't feel the sting that they'd never come back. I shouldn't think about all the other conversations, about lying on the roof of the dorm on a hot summer night, trying to find stars through all the light pollution of the city. I used to rest my head on Rhyland's shoulder, his fingers stroking slow circles across my hip when Noah wasn't around to get pissed.

I swallowed, trying to push down the memory.

"You were asking the girls for favors," Rhyland observed. "What do you need?"

As if he was going to help.

"I wouldn't say *asking,* and I wouldn't say *favors,*" I shot back. "Eventually, I'll have something to offer."

"Will you?" Rhyland tilted his head to one side, studying me. "This place is going to be bad for you, Brianna."

He said the words flat, deadpan. Unlike Noah, it didn't sound as if he took any joy in the idea.

"I didn't think it was a spa day," I shot back. "But if those girls run things in here, I think I'll be just fine. That punch was a joke."

"You don't know anything," Rhyland said. He wasn't smiling anymore. "You don't know how to survive in here."

"I'll make friends."

"No, you won't."

He sounded so definitive that I rolled my eyes. I was about to point out that he used to like me just fine. But just then, an alarm sounded. I tensed at the two chimes, wondering what it meant. Rhyland watched me, clearly waiting for me to ask, but I didn't want to owe him even the smallest bit.

I sat on the edge of the bed and began to unlace my shoes. I didn't even have any clean clothes; the other prisoners all wore dark sweats. Noah probably did intend to come back for me tomorrow, and this was his way of softening me up.

He'd searched me himself, probably taking sick pleasure in it as his hands patted brusquely across my body, shoving inside my pockets, running his fingers along my waistband. I had to bite my lip to keep from feeling anything, from remembering the loving way he used to caress me, when I believed he cared. Fucking stupid heart.

The overhead lights suddenly shut off. Fainter lights illuminated the catwalk outside, so there was still no real privacy.

Through the darkness, Rhyland still watched me.

"You're as creepy as Noah," I told him. "Why are you staring at me?"

"Do you want me to turn my back?" he asked, and I frowned at his words. As if he'd turn his back on me for good if that was what I wanted and not because he was a fucking traitor.

"Really?" I demanded. "Were you going to look out for me, Rhy?"

A memory rose in my mind of one of my first nights at the academy, when I was just a little girl. My mom had tried to keep me out of the angels' hands, moving us around constantly. Stroking my hair at night once, she'd whispered to me, *You're too special for this war, Brianna. I won't let them make you into another sacrifice.*

The day the angels snapped her neck in front of me was also my first day of school.

I'd crawled under my bed that first night in the dorm, so terrified that someone was going to snap *my* neck too, and Rhyland crawled under there with me. That was the kind of crazy that he used to be.

"You're always so tough, Brianna," he said. "Tell me you don't want me to look out for you. Tell me you're fine on your own."

His voice was taunting. So why did it feel like I'd be damning myself if I told him I didn't want him anywhere near me?

I rolled over onto my side, pulling the blanket over my shoulder. I refused to play his games.

Rhyland laughed and laughed, the noise eerie in the darkness.

CHAPTER NINE

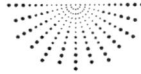

B *rianna*

I WOKE to the sound of metal banging all through the prison and glaring lights blazing down into my cell from the ceiling overhead.

"Go away," I mumbled, pulling the blanket over my head.

"Wake up, sleepyhead," crooned a sing-song voice in the next cell.

Fuck. I definitely wasn't ready for this day.

Someone banged the bars of my cell, making a clanging sound. "Up!" barked a voice. "Five minutes!"

"Five minutes until what?" I muttered to myself, throwing off the blankets.

"Group shower," Rhyland said, gripping the bars between our cells and grinning at me. "Then it's time for breakfast, and in case you're wondering, just because we're in a paradise doesn't mean we eat like the angels."

"I didn't expect to," I said, stretching and tucking the blankets up around my bed because I had nothing else to do, and the other prisoners were doing the same thing.

A minute later, a single, loud knock echoed through the jail. Every lock sprung open, and the cell doors slid back. I stepped out onto the walkway between the cells and found myself face to face with Rhyland. For a second, I had nothing to say. Somehow, it was different facing him with no bars between us. We stared at each other for a long moment, and it set in that this was real. I was in the fucking angel penitentiary.

And my former crew was here, too.

"How long have you been here?" I asked. I wasn't sure if asking someone what he did to get himself thrown in jail would get my ass kicked, and I wasn't ready to start another brawl just yet.

"You know how long," he answered. His smirk was gone for once, and he glowered at me from under lowered brows.

"I do?"

Before he could answer, someone yelled for us to march, and everyone turned and started toward a door at the end of the walkway. When we reached it, we were herded through. Rhyland wasn't kidding—we really did have group showers. Thank fuck they separated the men and women. Every two minutes, a whistle sounded, and the women under the showerheads went to get towels while a new batch got their two minutes. I wasn't a germophobe, but I sure as fuck liked more than two minutes to shower.

I noticed a few girls taking their sweet time before ceding their spot to the next person. I aimed for one with a meek looking girl under it, figuring she'd jump out right when the whistle blew. I was right, which gave me confidence. I'd have this shit down in no time. The way I figured it, Halftown was pretty much the same thing as prison, minus the bars. Shitty food, limited hot water, overcrowding, lots of assholes.

I'd barely rinsed the soap away before the whistle blew on the quickest two minutes of my life. I stepped out, noticing my cellmates from the night before staying under even as a chorus of grumbling went through the crowd.

"You got a problem with us?" Anna asked, spreading her arms while hot water streamed down on her back. "Come at me, bitch. I dare you."

No one moved.

I could see how this worked, too. If I was smart, I'd suck up and try to get on the good side of these bitches, make life easy for myself. But I wasn't one to grovel, and I sure as hell wasn't going to join their reign of terror. Instead, I went to get my towel and joined a group of women who'd already showered.

"So, guess those are the prison princesses," I said. "They run this place from the inside and get whatever they want?"

The other prisoners shied away from me, turning away to pull on their clothes. When I looked around, my clothes were gone, along with the rest of the laundry. Fine. If I was going to make alliances, I had to show these people I was one of them now. I grabbed a set of prison garb from the shelves bolted to the wall, each of them stacked with clean, folded prison uniforms. After slipping into a pair of sweatpants and a loose shirt like everyone else, I tried again.

"So, does anyone else know how I could get a message out of here?" I asked. "There's gotta be a way that doesn't involve the prison princesses."

"There's not," said a waifish little girl who couldn't be a day over sixteen and couldn't possibly have committed a crime worthy of prison. "Unless you know a guard, you can't slip anything out, and they're the only ones who know the guards."

"What are you going on about, Mouse?" Anna asked, butting between us. She plucked the uniform out of the girl's hands and dropped her wet towel in their place.

"N-nothing," the girl said, her face flushing as she turned and scurried to the laundry to dump the towel. She didn't even cast a backwards glance at me, and no one else would meet my eyes, either. Apparently, getting on the bad side of the prison princesses was a bad idea, and by making enemies of them, I'd made myself toxic to the other inmates. Whoops.

I didn't blame the others for turning away from a newcomer. They didn't know me, and they had to cover their asses and look out for themselves to survive in this place.

"You better watch your back, newbie," Erelah said, shoving past me and knocking me with her shoulder so hard I nearly went sprawling. "Or you might wake up with a knife in it."

I could've thrown down, but I decided to be the bigger person here. If I started a brawl in the shower, they'd probably send me to solitary like Beckett. I needed to find a way to get my message to Gemma, and that wouldn't happen if I couldn't see anyone. I just didn't know how I was going to do it if no one would talk to me.

I tossed my towel in the laundry chute and headed for the door, trying to keep myself from getting discouraged. When I stepped out the door of the shower room, Rhyland was leaning against the wall, looking bored. Seeing me, he straightened and fell into step beside me.

"Stalk much?" I asked, but I wasn't as annoyed as I pretended. It was a relief to see a familiar face, even if it was one that had cut and run, leaving me without a backwards glance.

"Don't flatter yourself," Rhyland said. "I have zero interest in you, Brianna."

"And yet, you're waiting outside the shower for me."

"Maybe I like to sneak a peek when the door opens."

"From what I remember, you had no trouble getting girls to take off their clothes for you."

"Sounds like someone's a little jealous," he said, flashing me a grin as we followed the crowd toward an open set of doors on the far side of the cellblock.

"Jealous of the poor girls you left sleeping, never to hear from you again? Not a chance."

"I was just testing out relationships, trying to find the right one for me."

"Right," I said, rolling my eyes. "Testing them for one night each?"

"Hey, when you know, you know," he said with a shrug. "Maybe I couldn't have what I wanted, so I had to be satisfied with what I could get."

"And what exactly was it you wanted?" I asked, annoyed at the way my heart pounded as I waited for his answer.

In response, Rhyland laughed that maniacal laugh that had always been so infectious. He grabbed my hand and dragged me through the doors in front of us into a large dining hall filled with prisoners. A few angel guards stood around the room, looking both watchful and slightly bored.

"Don't dally," Rhyland sang. "There's someone here who's been dying to see you."

"How would you know?" I asked, trying to balk. "You've been alone in your cell all night."

Rhyland tightened his grip and dragged me along. "Because some-one's allowed back into gen pop today," he said, tapping his forehead. "I know these things. Twin bond, y'know?"

"Beckett?" I asked, my throat going dry when I tried to swallow.

"Who else?" Rhyland asked, towing me to a table across the room where a familiar figure sat. But when Beckett looked up, I didn't see the boy I'd grown up with. I saw a man with a jagged scar marring his handsome face and hatred burning in his once-friendly eyes.

CHAPTER TEN

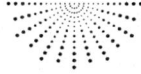

B*rianna*

"Take a seat, sweetheart," Rhyland crooned. My legs had stopped moving, but Rhyland pushed me down onto the seat across from Beckett.

Beckett stared at me for a few long seconds. His green eyes were both mesmerizingly beautiful and full of threat.

I couldn't say a damn word. That gaze drove every coherent thought out of my head, and randomly replaced it with a series of memories of Beckett. While Rhyland had comforted me that first night at the academy, Beckett had ignored me. He'd barely spoken to me for the first few months I was there, even though Rhyland and Noah had adopted me. The four of us had been inseparable. Beckett had joked around with Noah and Rhyland—he had a devilish sense of humor to go with his devilish streak—but he was so reserved and icy around anyone else that he was terrifying.

Then some idiot had pushed me off one of the training obstacles.

He'd almost really hurt me, and Beckett had done his level best to take his head off. After that, I'd told Beckett he had to stop being an ass and admit that we were friends.

And he had.

Too bad it wouldn't be that easy this time around, from the looks of it. Just like with the prison princesses, I couldn't look scared.

"Hey, friend," I said lightly, flashing him a smile. "It's been a while."

Rhyland sat in the seat beside me and buried his face in his hands. "You have always been shit at reading situations, Bri. It's painful to watch, really. You give me the worst case of second-hand embarrassment—"

Beckett's gaze flickered from me to him. "Shut up, Rhyland."

Then his gaze pinned me again. "What do you have to say for yourself, Brianna?"

His voice was low and cool.

Rhyland cupped his hand over his mouth and stage-whispered, "This is your chance to come up with a *brilliant* explanation for how you made it out of the heist at the courthouse and left us behind to suffer."

"What?" I glanced between them all. "You guys made it out. I saw you do it."

"Wrong answer," Beckett said. He glanced at the guards, then leaned close to me. "For old time's sake, I'd—"

"Oh no." I held my hand up, cutting him off. "You're forgetting that I know you. I know you're about to say some very scary things, and I'd love to play your little game because I know how important it is to you to feel dangerous and powerful and blah blah blah. I wish your mom had hugged you enough, but here we are."

Beckett's jaw tightened in a way that should've sparked fear in my heart, but I was getting pissed off now too.

Beside me, Rhyland hooted with laughter, then slapped his hand down on the tabletop. "Here we go."

I pointed a finger at Beckett. "But I can't, because *you are talking nonsense.* I never abandoned you. You assholes abandoned *me.*"

God, there was the faintest crack in my voice when I said *you aban-*

doned me that broke into my badassery routine. But I really had been devastated when they ditched me like the weak link, like we'd never been friends at all. I'd spent a fucking year questioning everything I'd ever known about my boyfriend and my two best friends.

Beckett's eyes narrowed. I got the feeling not a lot of people interrupted him with their amateur psychoanalysis.

"I think we need to recap," Rhyland said, clapping his hands together. The man was enormous and built and sexy in a terrifying way, but he still had the light-hearted energy from our younger days. Like a male cheerleader who was capable of doling out massive amounts of pain with a boyish grin and a wisecrack.

"Yeah, let's do that," Beckett said.

Just then, another bell sounded. Everyone pushed up from the tables, heading toward the serving station for breakfast. Everyone but us.

There was no way I was walking away from the twins now, before I'd gotten the explanation I'd waited three years for.

"What's going on?" Anna stalked over to us, followed by the other two. Anna twined her arms around Beckett's neck, and Erelah ran her hand up his arm.

"Oh, of course," I said. I should've known that the prince of psychos would have found a harem's worth of the most poisonous females I'd ever met.

Beckett didn't even spare them a glance. "Not now."

Hurt flashed across Erelah's face. Anna, though, just gave me a dark look over Rhyland's head. *"You're dead,"* she mouthed at me.

Then the three of them sashayed off, cutting into the cafeteria line. "Thanks for saving my spot!" Anna said loudly for the benefit of a guard, who did not appear to give a shit.

Rhyland shook his head. "Typical. Making friends everywhere you go."

"Yeah, this is pretty typical too," I shot back.

"Walk me through the day we robbed the Hall of Justice," Beckett said. "From what I remember, that morning you were freaking out

49

that Gemma wasn't going to live much longer if you didn't get a fast infusion of cash."

Rhyland and Beckett exchanged a glance, as if that meant something to them.

That was true. I'd almost forgotten that morning, but I'd had a tough time waking Gemma up. She had been failing fast. She'd skipped so many doses of her medication that she needed treatment in the hospital to stabilize her, but no one would take her until I could pay. I'd been freaking out, and Rhyland had wrapped me up in a hug that lifted my toes off the floor. Beckett told me to get my head in the game. He was always curt before a job, but then he'd said, "We'll take her as soon as we're done."

Instead, weeks later when I managed to scrape up the money, I'd carried a pale-faced, slack-jawed Gemma to the hospital myself, staggering under her weight. Because they'd left us to deal with her illness on our own.

"Right," I said, shaking my head to clear it. "We'd been casing the place together. I distracted the guard, Noah disarmed the alarm systems, the two of you knocked out the guard and went in first while I stashed his body."

We'd left him alive. No one thought humans or Nephilim could take down a full-powered angel, but we could. We'd felt unstoppable back then.

"As always," Rhyland put in. Rhyland and Beckett really did seem to have a 'twin sense' that was invaluable in committing felonies.

"As always, I was left cleaning up, you mean?" I replied. It was weird how I fell right back into talking to them like we used to, even though everything had changed. "Noah and I followed you two in."

Gemma used to be our lookout sometimes—even though crime made her queasy—but without her, we'd decided we couldn't afford to give up someone to be lookout. The four of us had needed to move fast, get the relics and get out of there. "Then we split up. Noah went to the hall to clean out the relics in the cases. I went to the judge's chamber to get the Grace there."

Nephilim died for the angels, and in return, they walked past glass cases displaying relics from Heaven that could change everything about their lives. It had seemed like poetic justice to steal from our angelic overlords.

If only it had worked.

"Then you triggered the alarm," Rhyland prompted.

"It was an accident," I said. "I hadn't realized there was a second guard that night. No one did. I tried to bring him down alone, and I slammed him into the display case—"

Noah had come running in to help me. I remembered the stricken look on his face as he faced me, my hands covered in golden blood, the angel slumped in front of me. He couldn't have been dead because Nephilim weren't strong enough to kill angels. I'd clung to that thought all these years. He'd looked so fucking *dead*.

"Get out of here," Noah had ordered, grabbing my arm and yanking me away from the body.

"The accidental part has always been in question," Beckett said dryly.

"You think I set it up?" I asked. I leaned across the table to hiss, "That I'd want to kill an angel? Come on…"

"If you even really killed an angel," Rhyland said. "You and Noah are the only ones who 'saw' that. But it brought a world of shit down on the two of us."

Only Noah hadn't seen it. He'd come in a second after.

I tried to convince myself it was some eye-for-an-eye shit. Some angel broke my mom's neck. Then I bashed a head in. Didn't it all come out in some terrible, violent wash?

As the alarms screeched, I'd run, knowing they'd all run, too. It was the plan. As I raced through Halftown, I'd heard the terrifying sound of wings beating overhead as the angels came for us. I'd expected the others to meet me at the safe house, but when I scrambled in there, I was alone.

When they never showed, I thought they'd taken the relics and split. I didn't make it out of there with a damn thing.

"I thought you took the money and ran," I said. "That you left me behind and went to another Halftown. That's what I would've done, *with* you guys, if it hadn't been for Gemma."

"What about the part where the angels caught up to you?" Rhyland asked, his voice cool. "When you pinned it all on us, told them where to find us, in exchange for freedom?"

"What?" I demanded. "That never happened."

"Not convincing." Beckett looked bored now. I knew that look. "I hoped you'd have some good explanation. Even *fuck you guys, I was always looking out for Gemma first.* That, I'd buy. I'd have some compassion."

"Sure you would," I said, rolling my eyes. "I didn't turn you guys in. I would never do that."

"Because you're such a nice person?" Rhyland's lips turned up.

"Nope. Definitely never said that," I replied. "Because you guys were my friends."

My family, even.

Beckett just stared at me, his eyes still cold and narrowed.

"When did you find out that Noah is an angel?" I asked.

"Ooh," Rhyland said. "I don't think we're to the *conversational* part yet. I think you're still pleading for your life and wellbeing in here with us, crow."

"They knew who you were, Brianna," Beckett said slowly. "Noah knew where you lived. So the only way you could've stayed free was if you cut some kind of deal."

Jesus, that was hard to argue with. I couldn't explain, though, because I didn't know. I was infamous for always slipping through the angels' hands when they almost caught up to me; that was why I was the best thief in Halftown.

"Whatever," I said. "I can't prove to you that I didn't do something. I guess Noah told you that I turned you in, right? Trying to get you to turn on me? And you're so fucking stupid that you believed him. What a pair of pathetic dickheads."

"Oh wow." Rhyland's gaze flickered from me to Beckett to back again. "Bold choices, Brianna."

I rose from my chair. "Believe what you want, but I'm not your enemy. I never was."

I wanted to storm off, but there was nowhere to go. When I turned, I was in a room full of unfriendly faces, all staring at me. I moved toward the now-empty breakfast line, only to realize I'd missed my chance to dine on a scrumptious bowl of oatmeal. Breakfast had closed.

I turned back, trying to take in the sea of faces, to sort out who might be a safe alliance for me.

But it was always Beckett and Rhyland who drew my gaze. Now, they were both looking right back at me. Beckett's gaze was unrelenting. Rhyland's smile was amused, no matter how hard his eyes were, as if he found some entertainment value in my attitude.

If I had to be in prison, that was bad enough.

Did I have to be in prison with my ex-best friends?

Fate was a heartless mistress.

CHAPTER ELEVEN

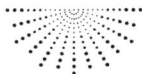

Brianna

I STOMPED toward the doors with everyone else, breakfast clearly not happening for me today. I was hungry as fuck, too, since the last time I ate was before leaving Gemma a full twenty-four hours ago. I desperately needed to get a message to her. The prison princesses obviously had it out for me. The other girls wouldn't help because they were scared of them. Which meant I needed to turn to a guy for help.

I'd never dated anyone but Noah—after having my heart ripped out, I wasn't too interested in trying again. Plus, I was busy caring for Gemma, and our little life was plenty for me. But that didn't mean I was above flirting to get some much-needed information.

I scanned the other inmates, looking for signs of interest. It didn't take long to find one of them eyeing me. He was tall and muscular, with ivory skin and jet black hair. Best of all, the other prisoners seemed to be giving him space, which meant he must be important.

He looked like the kind of guy who intimidated people by bashing skulls for fun. He gave me a slow smile when our eyes met, his gaze taking its sweet time roaming over my prison sweats before returning to mine.

I squeezed past a couple other girls to get to him. "Hey," I said. "I'm new here."

"You don't say," he drawled. His eyes were molten black, like the surface of flowing lava that turns black and just hints at the fire beneath. I'd never seen anything like them, and I faltered for a second before regaining my composure.

"Brianna," I said, holding out a hand.

He took my hand slowly, and I nearly yelped at how hot his skin was against mine. It was like dipping my hand into boiling water. I tried not to react, but something must've shown on my face, because he grinned wider. "Call me Shade."

"Okay, Shade," I said, dragging my fingers from the inferno of his hand. "I was wondering if you could point me in the right direction to find something I need."

"I've got just what you need," he said with a lazy grin. The prison princesses gave us a wide berth as they passed, and I decided I'd definitely chosen the right guy to befriend.

"A connection to get a message out of here?" I asked, quirking a brow.

He laughed.

"So?"

"Who you got on the outside?" he asked.

"A friend," I said with a shrug. "I just want her to know where I am, so she doesn't think I'm strung up on the walls of Paradise 12 as a warning."

"If she's smart, she's already checked there," he said, smiling like a psycho at the thought. "If *you're* smart, you won't keep friends on the outside. You wanna survive this place? Care about only one person —yourself."

"So, you don't know who could get a message out?"

"There's a couple guys who like to suck the guard's dick for special favors," he said, glancing behind me with a smirk. "Bet they could do that for you."

Before I could turn to see who he was looking at, a strong arm fell around my shoulders.

"What am I going to do with you?" Rhyland asked, dragging me away from Shade. "We leave you alone for two seconds, and you make friends with a fucking demon? What's wrong with you?"

A demon? Well, fuck me sideways. Was that the reason for the scalding touch and strange eyes? I knew demons were mortal enemies of the angels, and therefore the beings Nephilim were created to destroy, but I'd never actually met one. I shivered, glancing back over my shoulder before getting my head in the game. I couldn't let my guard down for even a second, no matter how surprised I was.

"Well, it's not like you were volunteering to help me," I said, throwing Rhyland's arm off. "Though according to Shade, you like to jerk off Noah for favors, so apparently you're the person to ask."

"Now she needs a favor," Beckett said, crossing his arms and glaring. "Of course."

"I just need to get a message to Gemma," I said. "It's not like I'm asking for a weapon or even a pack of smokes."

"Gemma?" Rhyland and Beckett exchanged glances again.

"Yeah, Gemma," I said, widening my eyes at them. "Remember her? Or did you conveniently forget about her, too?"

"In case you didn't notice, we're in a fucking prison," Beckett growled, leaning in so close our noses almost touched. "So forgive us for not sending a greeting card."

"Wait a minute," I said. "You've been in prison since... Shit."

Realization dawned then. When I never saw them again, the cold sense of being abandoned had crept into my soul. But they hadn't left me high and dry. They'd been caught. They hadn't disappeared to another Halftown, getting rich off the spoils of the heist while I scraped by to feed myself and Gemma. They'd been here all along, believing that Noah had let me go free in exchange for ratting them out.

"Thanks to you," Beckett said. "So tell me again why we should help you out?"

I sighed, wanting to tell them to just forget it. But I couldn't do that to Gemma. I needed to let her know where to find the Grace, which meant I needed these assholes to help me. They might hate me, and never believe the truth, but that hardly mattered now. What mattered was getting her some help.

"You wouldn't really be helping me," I said, hoping that would make the idea a little more palatable for them. "You'd be helping Gemma."

They shared one of those meaningful looks. She'd never done anything to them. Hell, she'd never hurt a soul in her life. She was the kind of person who would carry a mouse outside rather than killing it.

"Who's been taking care of her up until now?" Beckett asked, narrowing his eyes at me in suspicion.

"I have," I said, rolling my eyes. "Try to keep up here, boys."

"You and who else?" he asked, still looking at me like I was the traitor they all believed me to be.

"No one," I said. "It's just me and Gemma. And she's really weak right now, and I need to let her know where she can get help." To my horror, emotion swelled in my chest, and I started to get choked up.

"You've been taking care of Gemma all by yourself," Rhyland said, sounding suspicious, too. "For three years? It took all four of us before."

"Yeah, well, *all four of us* aren't around anymore. There's just me."

"How?" Beckett asked, frowning down at me.

I shrugged. "I did what I had to do."

The twins glanced at each other one more time, and I swore I'd kick one of them in the shins next time they locked me out of their silent communication like that.

"Okay," Rhyland said at last. "I'll get her a message."

"Thank you," I said, throwing my arms around his neck before I could think better of it. I was surprised at how much stronger he'd gotten, filling out his already fit form even more. It had been a long time since I'd been that close to a man, and damn if it didn't make my heart beat a little faster and warmth swell inside me.

There had always been a spark between us—really between all of us—but I'd been Noah's girl, so nothing had ever happened. But I'd always gotten the feeling that if I hadn't been with Noah, either of the twins would have happily filled his role.

"Damn, Bri," Rhyland said, but he took a second to feel me up before pushing me away. "Someone's gonna put a hit out on me if you keep feeling me up like that. I know I'm irresistible, but you gotta try."

"Riiiight," I said, rolling my eyes. "I'll do my best."

I noticed more than a few guys eyeing us as they passed, though.

"So, uh, what's going on with that?" I asked, cutting my eyes toward a leering inmate as he passed.

"You're hot, you're new, and you're showing interest in a guy," Beckett gritted out. "Which means you're available."

"Um, no," I said, shaking my head.

"In here, that's what it means," Rhyland said. "But don't worry, Brianna. They won't mess with you."

"How do you know?" I seriously doubted he could prevent every single guy in a prison this big from harassing me.

"Because you're ours," Rhyland purred, leaning in with a Cheshire grin. "Only we can mess with you."

"I'm yours?" I demanded. "I don't remember agreeing to that." I planted my hands on my hips and refused to budge, even when his face was so near I could see the golden flecks in his green eyes.

"I don't remember giving you a choice," Rhyland said. "You're ours because we said so."

"How about no," I said. "I'm not going to be your punching bag so you can get revenge for some imagined wrong I did you."

"You asked for a favor," Beckett said with a shrug.

"Seriously? This is the price of getting a note to Gemma?"

"I said I'd help," Rhyland retorted. "I never said it was free."

"Fine," I said. "If you want to play this game, I guess I'll have to play."

"I like to play," Rhyland said, chuckling.

"Come on," Beckett said. "We've got training. You'll join our group, Brianna."

"You're going to kill me, aren't you?" I asked, glaring between them.

Rhyland threw his head back and laughed that maniacal laugh that gave me chills.

Beckett smirked. "Sometimes accidents happen."

"Fine," I said, cocking an eyebrow at them. "Do your worst. But you'll never get the better of me."

CHAPTER TWELVE

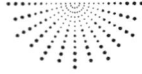

R *hyland*

As I LEANED against the bars between our cells, all I could think was that I should hate Brianna, but holy hell, that girl looked ridiculously good, even in the standard issue black sweats for training.

She finished pulling the sweatshirt over her head and cocked an eyebrow at me. "Are you going to babysit me twenty-four-seven?"

"If you're lucky." I stuck my hands in my pockets and pushed the sweatpants a little further down my hips, and her gaze flickered to follow the motion.

No matter where we were, there was still something hungry in her gaze. Brianna was never satisfied—not that she should have been. She always wanted more, better, and it wasn't because she was greedy. It's because we'd had nothing all our lives.

Until we found each other.

Things had never gotten physical between us because she was Noah's girl, but I'd always felt a bond between us. I used to be able to explain it away as us being friends. That was why I felt lighter, happier when she was around. Now we definitely weren't friends, and yet, just having her here again made me feel happier than I'd been in years.

"So what are you and Beckett going to do to me?" she asked as she bent over to pull on her sneakers. "Is there some dastardly plan to break me?"

"I think we're just going to wing it." I looked her over, feeling like I should let her stick out like the newb she was, but I just couldn't do it. "None of the girls wear their sweatshirts out there."

"Well, I don't have a t-shirt like you do." She frowned, flashing a jealous look at the black t-shirt that clung to my pecs and shoulders, her gaze lingering. Then she got it and pulled her sweatshirt back off. Now she just wore black pants that clung to the curve of her hips and a black sports bra that exposed her narrow, taut waist. The diamond blinking at me from above her belly button was new.

"Did you steal the rock?" I asked, nodding toward her midriff.

"It's fake." She ran her fingertips over it absently. "Most of my money's gone to Gemma's medicine, just like old days. What about you? Any new piercings?"

I shook my head, ignoring her tone. I couldn't decide if it was teasing or challenging. "I took mine out a little after we got here," I said. "I kept getting into fights, and people were very devoted to ripping them out, and my flesh along with them."

I gave her a meaningful look, hoping she'd get the message and pull the belly button ring out before someone else tried to. But she just frowned. "Rhy, I'm sorry—"

"I don't want to fucking hear it," I cut her off. If our shared past held true, I'd cave if she apologized. I forced a grin, though tension tightened my chest when she started to apologize. "You're sorry? Don't tell me with words, Bri. Show me."

"Any day, you two. Don't want to be late," Beckett said impatiently, heading out into the hall. He glanced at Brianna, his jaw stiff. "You'll find there are actual consequences in here. Good as you generally are at avoiding them."

She scoffed. "I keep waiting for whatever you two are going to do, but this is it, isn't it? Listening to the two of you whine for an eternity behind bars is the ultimate punishment."

Beckett's jaw tensed even more. I knew from the way he moved that he was going to close the distance between him and Brianna, but I wasn't sure what the hell he was going to say or do once he reached her. Beckett was a good guy, but he hid it well—he acted like a fucking psycho half the time. Being locked up in here hadn't brought out the best in him, either.

I slung my arm over her shoulders, putting my body between the two of them as I walked with her down the hall. "So how are you going to make your little double-cross up to us, anyway? I've got some ideas now that you're our girl. But I'm curious what you can think up."

She rolled her eyes. "You don't need me. Apparently half the girls in here want to fuck the two of you."

"Just half?" I feigned hurt.

She shook her head. No matter how prickly she was with every word that came out of her mouth, she subtly leaned into me when my arm was around her shoulders.

The three of us headed out into the yard. Most folks were clustered in groups of eight. She looked around, her eyes keen, the breeze ruffling her hair as an alarm sounded. We all started running in our groups, warming up. She automatically fell into stride like we were back at the damn academy.

"Why is it just the three of us?" she asked as we rounded the yard for the end of our second lap. Beckett had set a hard pace, and we were all panting.

"No one else can keep up with us," Beckett said.

"No one else *wants* to be on our team," I clarified. "They think this dude's a psycho. For some reason, people are afraid of us."

"The chaos twins strike again," Brianna said lightly. That was what people had called us at the academy—sometimes affectionately, but only in the case of Noah, Gemma, and Brianna.

One of the guards stopped us with a raised hand. Beckett rolled his eyes as he slowed to a stop, the other teams running past us. I glared at Beckett as I reminded him, "Try not to get tossed into solitary."

"Oh, I'm not about to miss any of the shit that's going down around here now," he promised me.

He might plan to stay out of solitary to torment Brianna, but I knew how protective he used to be of her. She'd very well be the reason he went back. I hoped, for his sake and everyone else's, that word had already gotten around from breakfast that Beckett and I had staked a claim before anyone had the chance to fuck with Brianna.

"You can train with the girls." The guard pointed Brianna to a group of girls running on the outer rim of the track, all of them talking easily like the three of us couldn't right now. Anna and Erelah and the rest of the nightmare gang were in that group.

"I don't mind staying with them," Brianna said.

"Do I look like I give a fuck what you want?" he demanded. "Go."

Brianna frowned, and the guard took a step toward her. Next to me, Beckett tensed, and Brianna's gaze flickered to him. He could pretend he didn't give a fuck all he wanted, but I was pretty sure she could read his posture.

"Got it," she said lightly. "See you boys around."

She turned and jogged toward the group of girls.

Beckett was in a mood as the two of us resumed our run. I could feel irritation rolling off him in waves. He was grumpy even by Beck's standards.

We went through our paces like usual: running, strength exercises, hand-to-hand combat training. They didn't trust us with weapons, but we were still preparing for war. It was all a reminder that in the end, we were still cannon fodder for the angels.

At least it was something to do, and it gave me a chance to hit someone.

By the time we lined up for hand-to-hand, Brianna had mud streaked across her cheek and in her hair, and fire in her eyes. She faced off with Anna, and I wondered whether it had been Anna or Brianna who had jostled others to make sure they fought each other.

In the distance, I could hear guards placing casual bets.

"Ready," one of the angels who instructed our training called over the loudspeaker.

I glanced past James, the face of the guy who stood across from me, to watch Brianna. I hadn't seen her in action in years. She'd been a badass little thing when we were at the academy. Everyone always underestimated her.

Quick as could be, Anna and the guy next to her switched places. Brianna stared at the six-foot-something asshole who stood in front of her now.

Then she grinned.

When the bell sounded, James came at me, and I punched him in the face, intent on getting him out of my way so I could keep an eye on Brianna. He went down on one knee and caught me around the waist. I slammed my fist into the side of his abs, still watching her over his shoulder. His fist jabbed my kidneys, and I grunted, stumbling back with him as we locked up, trying to find openings to hit each other.

But most of my attention was on Brianna as the big guy went for her. Anna and the guy she was supposed to be fighting were just watching them, too; half the line had paused to watch the fight. Even the angels were watching. Brianna danced Gracefully in the fight, staying out of his reach as much as possible. She suddenly darted forward under his arms and hooked his ankle with hers as she slipped past him. He was too slow to catch her, and he almost went down. He tried to hit her, but she was already out of reach, spinning around.

James hit me across the face again. Oh, fuck this. I threw him over my shoulder and then dropped on top of him, grabbing his face to hold him down so he would stop distracting me.

Brianna danced back, avoiding the big guy's fists and looking for her opening. Before she could find it, some bitch tripped her. She stumbled, and her opponent closed the distance between them, punching her right in the face. Rage tightened my chest, and my grip tightened on James, who let out a muffled groan.

Brianna hit the ground hard, but she was already placing her hands by her shoulders. I'd seen her do this move enough times to know she was going to kick over and somersault back up into a fighting position. But one of the girls stepped on her hair. Brianna winced as she started to roll up, then jerked to a stop. The guy stepped over her, about to drop his massive weight onto her. Then he'd be able to hit her in the face and head at his leisure.

I started to get to my feet, but Beckett ground out, "Wait for it." He and his opponent had stopped sparring to watch.

"I'd rather that pretty face of hers didn't get ruined on day one," I said.

James tried to throw me, and this time I accidentally punched him too hard and knocked him out. His head slumped against the ground, his eyes fluttering closed. I shook out my hand as I bounced up to my feet.

Brianna kicked her attacker in the nuts, then grabbed the ankles of the girl who had stepped on her hair and yanked her feet out from under her. As she came down, Brianna used her legs as leverage to throw herself to her feet. She elbowed the bitch in the face, then rebounded on the guy. Grabbing his shoulders while he was still bent over grieving his testicles, she kneed him in the face. She didn't stop after the first time, either.

By the time she let him drop, the same guard who had sent her over to Anna and company in the first place had pulled his baton.

"Walk away," he warned her.

There was a nasty bruise forming across her cheekbone already and blood at the corner of her lip, dribbling down her chin, but she grinned as she raised her hands to her shoulders in a sign of backing off.

That's my girl.

"Join your fuckup friends," the angel told her, pointing his baton in our direction. He spoke like a man who had just lost some money—not that angels were supposed to care about such things. "I'll be keeping an eye on you, psychobitch."

"Will do," she said lightly, before sauntering toward us.

"Told you," Beckett muttered, too quietly for her to hear. "I don't trust that girl for shit, but I trust her to kick some ass."

I laughed out loud at the two of them. Brianna still kicked ass, it was true. And Beckett still hated her—or at least he was trying to.

"Welcome back to where you belong," I said, throwing my arm around Bri's shoulder. "With us, all the damn time."

"Lucky me," she muttered. An alarm went off, the same blast of noise that measured all our days.

"Training's over," I told her. "Lucky *them*."

"Go get cleaned up," Beckett ordered.

I could tell from the way she looked at me that Beckett ordering me around didn't pass unnoticed. Someone had to stay with her, though. Apparently word hadn't gotten around that she was ours, and someone else would surely try to mess with her.

Beckett moved stealthily across the yard, no doubt to have a discussion regarding just that with the guy who had tried to kick her ass. The guy saw him and made a wide circle around Beckett, trying hard to blend in with the crowd leaving the yard. I jerked my head at Brianna, and she walked with me back to our cell.

"How's the face?" I asked, pressing my fingers against her cheekbone to probe the bruise.

She winced, grabbing my wrist and wrenching my hand away. "It hurts. It hurts worse when you fucking poke it."

"I know." I grinned at her as I stroked my thumb lightly over the bruise again.

She caught my hands in hers, then held onto then this time as she dropped our hands between us.

"Beck and I will make sure that guy pays for hurting you," I told her, serious for once.

"I think I made him pay already," she said, a smirk twisting her lips. Her gaze met mine, her eyes the most mesmerizing shade of emerald.

"Doesn't matter. No one fucks with what's ours."

She rolled her eyes, and I caught her chin between my thumb and finger, turning her face up to mine. "You might find you like it, Brianna."

Her lips parted, no doubt to tell me off.

I leaned in and covered her mouth with mine before she could.

Her palm pressed against my shoulder as if she were going to shove me away. Instead, her lush lips softened against mine, her hand slipping up until her fingers gripped the back of my neck.

I teased the tip of my tongue across her upper lip, and her lips parted against mine. I wrapped my hands around her narrow hips, about to pull her body close to mine. Kissing Brianna felt like a wave of heat washing over my body after being cold for too long.

I meant to remind her that she was *ours,* but as her breath hitched in her chest at my touch, I realized I was fucking *hers.*

"What the hell is this?" a rough voice demanded from the door of the cell.

Noah.

Fan-fucking-tastic.

Brianna started to pull away, but I wrapped my arm tighter around her waist and kissed her one last time before I straightened, letting her go. Her lips were red, her cheeks flushed, her eyes wide. The sight of her made my cock even harder.

Too bad I had to look away from her and into the furious face of my best friend-turned-tormentor.

CHAPTER THIRTEEN

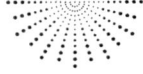

B *rianna*

NOAH'S FINGERS were tight around my bicep as he *helped* me down the hall. He came to a halt in front of a set of doors, looking dead into the camera as he waited for us to be buzzed through. I tried to jerk my bicep out of his grip, but his response was to grip the nape of my neck with his other hand, his body pressing against my back.

"It doesn't take you long to return to old habits, does it, Brianna?" he murmured in my ear, his voice dark.

No matter how much he hated me, I suddenly realized that the hardness I felt against my ass wasn't a nightstick. *One* part of him didn't hate me, anyway.

"Jealous, love?" I cooed. "That's not a good look for an angel. It's not very dignified."

That was what the angels cared about most, how they appeared, how much they were *adored*.

His mouth dipped closer to my ear, and despite myself, my thighs tightened, a sudden ache throbbing between them. I knew how good that mouth could be, no matter how bad Noah was.

"Why do you try so very hard to make me angry when you know what I can do to you?"

I felt my lips twitch in a mirthless smile. "Does it matter what happens to me when I'm in here and Gemma is dying?"

Once I got that message to her, once she had the Grace, she had to run. Noah would have a tail on her. She'd need to be clever.

But with her health restored, she would actually—for the first time —be able to take care of herself.

The doors buzzed open, and Noah barked a cynical laugh, the sound even rougher and more grating that the buzz of the doors.

"Yeah, sweetheart, you'll find that it matters," he warned me. He steered me down an empty hallway and into an interrogation room.

"I don't magically feel more chatty with you than I did yesterday," I warned him.

This room looked like a mirror image of the interrogation room I'd be in yesterday: a table bolted to the ground, a pair of chairs.

But this time, there was something glittering on the table.

A knife, with a long, dangerous blade and a jeweled handle.

My heart froze in my chest. I almost took a step back, but Noah was there, filling the doorway. He pushed me further into the room, closing the door behind him.

I lunged for the knife, grabbing the hilt. Fear was wild in my chest. He was going to torture me, I knew that, and I would kill him first.

I whirled, the knife clutched in front of me, already in fighting stance.

Noah stared at me from the doorway, crossing his arms over his powerful chest. The faintest smile slipped across his lips. "Typical Brianna. I heard you put on quite a show in the yard today."

"What were you planning on happening with the knife, Noah?" I demanded. Fuck me. My instincts were too quick sometimes; I'd seen the knife and I'd gone for it.

But Gemma didn't know where the Grace was. If Noah intended to torture me, I should have just suffered and survived long enough to get the message to her. Now that I had the knife, it was hard to go backwards. I'd grabbed it with every intention to kill him rather than let him torture me, even though I knew killing him—here, in their prison—was a death sentence. If I even managed to take Noah down, I'd never get out of here.

And I was suddenly not sure I could take Noah at all, as he leaned against the door, his posture perfectly relaxed. It didn't seem to bother him in the slightest to be trapped in here, apparently weaponless, while I had a blade. His confidence was disconcerting.

"Exactly that," he said, his voice cool. "I knew that if you saw a weapon, you'd grab it, you bloodthirsty bitch."

His smile widened just a little, and I could've sworn it was almost affectionate. Only Noah would call someone a bloodthirsty bitch as an endearment.

"Did you have a plan for step two, genius?" I asked. "I don't want to fight you."

"Yes, you do," he accused. "But I don't intend to fight you."

I glanced down at the knife in my hand. I usually held a knife lightly in the moments before I struck, ready to flip my grip if I needed to throw it again. But my fingers tightened around the hilt, and I couldn't get them to relax. I frowned, jerking my gaze up to Noah, afraid that I was letting my attention slip with him.

"That's the blade of Uriel," he said casually. "Well, one of them. Not *the* blade of Uriel; that one is valuable, and you'd probably find a way to walk off with it. But we've been able to duplicate the original."

"I'm touched by your faith in my thievery skills," I said, trying to drop the blade back on the table. I couldn't pry my fingers off the hilt.

"Oh, I have faith in you for every rotten thing, Brianna," he promised me.

I thought the Blade of Uriel was a myth. Maybe it was. Maybe this was just some psychological game, and it was my own foolish mind convincing me I couldn't just fling the blade from my hand. Possibly flinging it right into Noah's damned chest.

"You aren't convinced it's real," he said. "Let's give it a try. Seeing is believing. Sit."

I narrowed my eyes. "Why shouldn't I just kill you now, since I have a knife in my hand and that's what you would expect?"

He raised his hand lazily, still leaning against the door, and curled two fingers toward himself. An invitation.

I hesitated. I didn't really want to kill him; I wanted to get out of here someday, somehow.

"If you're not going to kill me, then sit the fuck down like I told you." His tone was impatient, as if he were beginning to fray just from the misery of being in a room with me.

"Cursing now," I noticed, as I reluctantly took a seat at the table.

"You always bring out the best in me," he said, jerking out the seat across from me. "Also? No one can see us in here. There's no recording. It's just you and me, sweetheart."

"Oh, so you can be yourself. Now I'm scared."

His lips parted. "Let's start with a gentle warm-up before we discuss the Grace, just so you can see how it works."

"I can hardly wait." My heart was beating frantically fast, but I leaned back in my chair, forcing my posture to mirror his. He looked relaxed, after all. Like the fucking king of the world, like all angels thought they were.

"Brianna," he said, his voice dropping low, laced with command. "I'll ask you a question, and you'll tell me the truth. If you start to speak a lie, the blade will find the inside of your arm. Reach the end of your lying sentence, and you'll cut yourself—not too deeply now, just a shallow cut."

He smiled. "The truth is your redemption. You always have choice not to spill your own blood."

"You're a fucking monster, Noah." Fear wrapped its fingers around my chest, squeezing tight.

I'd heard stories—but I'd dismissed them as superstition that the angels probably perpetrated to spread terror—of the kinds of damage that angels forced people to inflict on themselves or tell the truth. People cut off their own fingers one-by-one, or drove the knife into their own guts, or cut their own throats. Grown men wept as they killed themselves rather than tell the truth.

71

Now suddenly, I knew those stories were all true.

"Warm up question one," he said, holding up three fingers and pressing his index finger back. "What happened that night? How did you kill that angel in the museum?"

"I didn't," I answered.

He glanced at the knife, still clutched tightly in my right hand, and he frowned slightly.

"Did Rhyland or Beckett kill the angel?" he demanded, pressing his second finger.

"I didn't think either of them did. Last I saw of them, they were running off all proud of themselves for getting one over on the winged fuckwads," I said. I flashed him a tight smile. "Remember how you used to call them that, too?"

He tilted his head to one side. I could see him thinking before he said slowly, "That night that we drove all night to get to the ocean. Did you mean it when you said you loved me?"

That motherfucker.

That night, we'd had a weekend of liberty from the academy. We still weren't supposed to leave Halftown, but we'd escaped. The four of us drove all night because we'd never seen the ocean before. Dawn had been rising when we waded into the freezing-cold water at the edge of the ocean, the wind like a slap, but it hadn't mattered. Something immense and beautiful, dangerous and wonderful all at the same time had stretched in front of us. Noah had been at my side, his arm around my waist. For once, I hadn't been surrounded by destruction. The ocean was the one thing bigger than our endless war. I'd thought my heart would overflow in that moment from how beautiful it was, how much it had overwhelmed me, how much I'd loved Noah for dragging us all out to the ocean in the first place.

Now I realized he must have seen it before. He hadn't really belonged in Halftown with us. The knowledge hit me like a punch in the gut. Everything he'd ever told me, it had all been a lie. He'd let me believe that he loved me, that we were sharing this indescribable moment of magic, but to him, it was nothing. I knew his betrayal would hit me in waves like this as over and over, I realized that everything we'd ever shared was a lie. I didn't want to admit how much it hurt, not after he'd broken my heart by leaving me behind like the trash angels thought we were. I couldn't bear to tell him that I really had loved him while he tortured me. I'd rather cut my own eyes out.

"No," I said.

My hand rose of its own volition. I tried to force it back down onto the table, and my forearm tensed so much that my whole arm began to tremble. My other hand turned palm up on the table, my bare arm against the cold metal tabletop as if I were waiting for blood to be drawn by a doctor.

I tried to focus on forcing my hand back down, but I couldn't do it. The cold, sharp edge of the blade rested lightly against my skin.

Noah's eyes sharpened. "Don't do it, Brianna."

I forced the lie in a whisper, because suddenly my voice couldn't rise any higher. Because shame and hatred and humiliation burned through me as he forced me to admit what a fool I'd been, that I'd loved him when I'd been nothing but a starry-eyed idiot he could fuck and then laugh about how he'd slummed it up with a Nephilim when he got back to his angel buddies. The fact that after all that, he could force me to humiliate myself again with this ego-stroke of a confession hurt more than anything. Because I knew in that moment, that no one who ever loved me could have been so cruel.

I forced the words past my numb lips. "I was never stupid enough to love you, Noah."

The blade slashed across my arm, and I gasped. The sudden cut was so sharp, so sudden, that it barely hurt at first as red blood welled up under the blade. Then suddenly, the cut was bleeding freely, and the pain came in a rush. I gasped at how much it hurt. I'd been cut in fights before, but this was different.

Everything hurt more as a captive.

Something resigned came over Noah's eyes. He leaned back, studying me curiously.

"It's time for you and I to have a conversation about that Grace," he said.

73

CHAPTER FOURTEEN

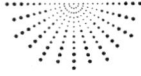

B *rianna*

I STOMPED INTO THE INFIRMARY, biting back the sobs of pain that threatened each time I let my concentration slip from the anger. I held onto it, treasuring and nursing it in my heart, knowing it was the only thing keeping me from blubbering like a baby. Uriel's blade must have been made of acid as well as metal, because the cuts burned like fire. Blood dripped from my fingertips to the polished cement floor. I hadn't given up the Grace without a fight, though I knew I was the only one who'd been hurt in that fight. Noah had no heart to hurt.

"There's a room on your right," said a bored looking angel who sat at a desk, playing solitaire on the surface screen.

I turned and walked in, hoping for a pillow that could muffle my sobs of pain. Instead, I found a room with two narrow beds. At one edge of the room, a hulking guy sat on a rolling stool leaning over a bloody hand mirror. He slowly drew a needle and thread through his skin as he stitched up a gash that ran down his forehead, through one eyebrow, and over his cheekbone. Suddenly, I remembered Beckett's scar, and a shudder of horror gripped me. Was that where he'd acquired the scar? At Noah's hand—probably for not ratting me out? No wonder he hated me.

"Gauze in the drawer," the guy said in a drawling voice I recognized as I took him in. Black hair, pale skin, broad shoulders, devil-may-care attitude. The demon I'd met my first day here—Shade. He was stitching up his own cut, which looked much deeper than mine. Blood dripped down his hands and onto the mirror as he worked.

"What happened to you?" I asked, opening a drawer and finding nothing bigger than a bandage for a paper cut.

"Ran into a doorknob," Shade said, sarcasm lacing his voice. "You?"

I held up my arm so he could see. "Got in a fight with a lawnmower."

"Damn," he said, glancing up and flashing me a grin that was made particularly gruesome by the blood covering half his face. "I'd hate to see the lawnmower."

"We have to stitch up our own wounds?" I asked, finding the roll of gauze at last.

"There's a surgeon," he said. "But he's shit with stitches. I like to keep my pretty face pretty, so I do it myself."

"I don't care about scars," I said. "Won't be my first, won't be my last."

"If you change your mind, I'm the best," he said, picking up a towel and wiping blood out of his eye. "I've had lots of practice."

"Any pain meds around?" I asked, wincing as I wrapped my arm.

Shade laughed mirthlessly. "You think they'd waste that on us? Now, if you don't mind, it's a little hard to concentrate with a smokin' hot angel-baby standing over me."

I rolled my eyes and sat down on one of the beds. It was basically a rubber exam table with a sheet wrapped over it. I really hoped no one ever had to spend a night in the infirmary, as there was no way anyone could sleep on that. It was obviously meant to deter people from wanting to stay longer than necessary. I watched Shade to keep my mind off my own pain. He flinched with every stitch when he went over his eyebrow, but otherwise, he showed no outward signs of the pain he must have been in. At last, he straightened, held up the mirror, and grinned at himself. A needle still dangled from his cheek.

"Looks pretty great, huh, angel-baby?" he said, flashing a grin as our eyes met in the blood-streaked mirror.

"Do not call me that."

"Whatever you say, angel-baby," he said, setting down the mirror. He tore open a packet of wipes and started cleaning his face. "That's what you are, isn't it? An angel's baby with some sucker human who fell for their savior bullshit."

"They were supposed to save humanity," I said, the words programmed into me since birth.

Shade turned away from the counter where he'd just done his own stitching, sans anesthesia. The stitches might not leave bad scars later, but they looked pretty fucking gnarly right now, black threads pulling tight against his inflamed skin. I tried not to show my horror at his appearance and the amount of pain he must be in right now.

He gestured to his face and then my arm and quirked an eyebrow. "And I guess you think I'm the bad guy here?"

"I don't think that," I said quietly.

He stood, turning his back to me while he mopped his blood off the counter with the stained towel. "Well, you should. I'm a demon, after all."

"So, where's this surgeon?" I asked, my own pain reminding me that I'd been here quite a while without anyone coming to check on me.

"You think they're going to wait on you like an angel?" Shade asked. "You met the surgeon. Nice guy. Likes to play cards with himself. Might be having a cocktail at his desk right about now."

"That's the surgeon?" I asked, skepticism filling me when I remembered his complete indifference to seeing me walk in, leaving a trail of blood all the way.

"That, or you can do it yourself," Shade said, tossing me a roll of black thread.

I caught it by instinct and stared down at the gauze wrapping.

Blood was already leaking through in one spot. "First time for every-thing," I muttered, unwrapping my arm.

Shade came over and took hold of my wrist, turning my arm slightly to examine the slashes. I gasped at the burning heat in his touch, but this time, he ignored it. "You know, I think you only need stitches in this one," he said, pointing to the deepest cut—the last one. The one that had finally broken me, forcing me to admit to Noah where I'd put the Grace.

"Well, that's a relief," I said. "You should see the socks I've tried to mend. My stitching looks more like an ax murderer's than a surgeon's."

"I thought you weren't worried about scars," Shade mocked. "Makes you look all tough, right?"

"I'm not worried about them," I said, pulling away from him.

"Good," he said, sitting down on the edge of the second bed. He leaned back, propping himself on his palms, and fixed me with a look of pure, smug challenge.

I took a deep breath and reached for the needle he'd used.

"Better wash that," he said, swinging his feet casually as he watched me. "Wouldn't want to get your boys' angel-baby tainted with demon blood."

I gritted my teeth and stood, reaching the sink set into the counter in one step. The room was tiny, not much more than the two beds, the stool, and the counter with drawers below and cabinets above.

"Alcohol in the cabinet to the left," Shade said. I opened it and pulled down a bottle of rubbing alcohol, which I dumped over the needle. Then, for good measure, I dumped it over my arm. Whatever that blade had added to it, I hoped disinfectant could clean it. The pain hit me like a wall of fire. I bit down on my tongue so hard I tasted blood just to keep from screaming.

"Damn," Shade said behind me, sounding truly impressed. "You're one crazy bitch."

I was so glad he couldn't see my face.

When I could draw a breath without screaming, I turned back from the sink. "So, I guess this is part of their torture, huh? Knowing that not only are they forcing us to injure ourselves, but that we'll have to keep suffering."

"What, is that not something your savior would do?" Shade asked, his eyes widening with innocence.

"Shut up," I muttered, fighting back a smile.

I sat down on the stool, braced my elbow on my knee, clenched my teeth and dug the needle into my skin. The pain nearly knocked me backwards and left me gasping for breath. I had no idea how Shade could sit there hardly blinking while he did this to his face. A pathetic whimper escaped me as I dragged the thread through my skin. Five stitches later, my breath came in panting little gasps, my eyes were watering, and my hands were shaking.

"Angels above, you're not going to make it in this place if you can't handle a little pain," Shade said, hopping off the bed and strolling over. He put a hand on my knee, wheeling the stool toward him as he knelt on the floor. The fever heat of his hand burned through my sweats, but I didn't protest when he took the needle. I'd held it together through all the cutting, but sticking a needle into my mangled skin was worse.

Shade hummed as he got a towel, rolled it up, and handed it to me. "Bite down," he said. "Screaming actually makes it hurt less. Especially if you scream obscenities at your *savior*, who did this to you."

I bit down on it. He sewed, and I screamed.

When he was done, he lifted me off the stool and lay me on the bed before I could protest. He sat down beside me, his head propped on his hand, so close to me that I could feel the heat coming in waves off his body. "Now, that wasn't so bad, was it?"

I couldn't help but let out a shaky laugh. "Piece of cake," I said. "I've had naps that took more out of me."

Shade grinned. "So, are those two angel-babies going to try to kick my ass for taking care of their girl when they weren't around?"

"I'm not their girl," I said, scowling at him.

"Did you tell them that?" he asked, cocking his good eyebrow.

"I tried," I said with a sigh. "And it's not like they wouldn't take care of me if they knew what had happened. They weren't there. They didn't *let* anyone hurt me." I had a ridiculous urge to defend the twins, little as they deserved it.

Shade cracked his knuckles one by one. "So, they are going to try to kick my ass."

"Don't tell me you're afraid of a couple *angel babies*, as you call us."

"Not afraid," he said, a bloodthirsty grin spreading across his lips. "I look forward to it."

"Has anyone ever told you that you're a little insane?"

"I have an excuse," he said, leaning forward and lowering his voice. "I'm a demon. We're the bad guys, remember?"

"I'm beginning to think it's not so black and white," I said, staring up into his eyes. They were almost black. But there were other colors, threaded through the darkness; I couldn't tell exactly what they were, but I couldn't stop trying. Suddenly, my heartbeat felt heavy and labored.

"Don't be so quick to change your mind, angel-baby," he murmured, leaning down, his face so close to mine that my breath caught in my chest. His eyes flicked to my lips. "If you were my girl, and someone cut you up that way, I'd pull out their intestines and feed them back to them."

I swallowed hard, but it was his nearness making my heart pound, not fear. Right about now, that punishment sounded too good for Noah. The girl who had loved him was long dead.

"What if they were an angel?" I whispered.

"If they were an angel," Shade said, slowly stroking my raven hair behind my ear. "I'd laugh while I did it."

"Okay, you're more than a little insane," I said, trying to laugh, trying to understand how I could have let myself trauma-bond with a fucking demon. This was not good.

"Don't worry, angel-baby," he drawled, chucking me under the chin like a child. "When I was done with him, I'd bring you back his heart as a souvenir."

"I'm afraid you'd be in for a disappointment," I said. "Noah doesn't have a heart."

Shade shrugged. "Then I'd bring you his dick."

CHAPTER FIFTEEN

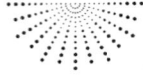

N *oah*

Brianna stashed the Grace somewhere on her way through Halftown, which I knew, but none of our searches turned up the stuff before I talked to her. I'd been hunting for it until the last minute, but I'd pushed it too far. I should've made her face the damned blade a little sooner.

If I didn't get the Grace in time, she was dead. It wasn't like she would've believed me if I'd warned her. I couldn't entirely blame her. She had no reason to trust or believe anything I said. The hate in that girl's eyes could've burned me alive. But I was hard-hearted enough to save her life.

Half expecting to find nothing, to find someone had already beaten me to the Grace, I reached inside her hiding place. Instead of a dusty floor, my fingers wrapped around a warm, pulsing orb.

I exhaled with relief as I slid the Grace into my leather bag and slung it over my shoulder. I felt eyes on me as I headed down the alleyway. Some Nephilim had seen me withdraw the Grace. I was still restless with tension after being face-to-face with that stubborn girl. I'd have loved if someone was so stupid as to try and hurt me. I could use the fight.

Instead of giving into temptation, I gritted my teeth and headed for the street—I'd fly rather than risk getting caught by a bunch of Nephilim gangsters. I risked doing too much damage to the buildings on either of me if I stretched my wings here. People in Halftown needed their homes, such as they were.

But the Nephilim were faster than I expected.

When I reached the end of the alley, two of them abruptly stepped in front of me. One of them held a gun in his outstretched hand. I turned, protecting the Grace with my body.

If I didn't deliver the Grace, Brianna was dead.

The gun roared in the confines of the alley as it kicked in the man's hand, which didn't stop him from squeezing off one, two, three rounds before I reached him. I knew the gun was just the distraction to slow me down, but I still had to deal with it. I grabbed the weapon, twisting it out of his hands as I mangled the barrel. He managed to squeeze off one last round, but I shoved him away before the bullet exploded in the now-broken gun. It blew up in his face as he stumbled backwards.

The other guy dove toward me with a devil's blade. The black metal shimmered as if it were alive.

I sidestepped it and grabbed his arm, smashing it across my knee as I brought my knee up, breaking his elbow. He screamed, but I kept control of his arm, reeling him toward me to get to the knife.

Before I was able to grab the blade from his fingers, I felt someone right behind me. I whirled, and a second demon's blade glanced across my side, ripping through my flesh. Fuck. Two demon's blades made this a much fairer fight—but worse, it meant trouble.

The second guy tried to close in on me as his friend, breathing heavily from the pain of the break, tried to get control of his knife again.

"I'm so glad you're here, friend," I told the guy with the knife. I really needed someplace to work out my emotions today. I waved him closer, an invitation, and stood waiting for them both to pick up their blades.

The two of them circled me as I stood waiting for them to press their attack.

The two of them rushed at me at once. Still mindful of the Grace in my bag, I grabbed the first one's arm, controlling the knife, as I ducked low. I threw out my leg as I whirled, tripping the second, and he stumbled forward, just as I drove the other's blade up. The second Nephilim's eyes went wide as he was impaled on his friend's knife. I ripped it out of his chest and used it to finish the first guy.

When the two bodies slumped dead on the ground, I stood, wrenched both blades from their chests, and studied the bloodied weapons.

War relic? Or were there Nephilim fighting on the demon side now? One more thing to investigate, as if I weren't busy enough. The war with the demons was already desperate.

Shaking my head, I left their bodies behind and stepped into the street before I soared into the air. Once I was safely airbound with the Grace, I called my boss, the Archangel Michael himself.

"I've got the Grace," I said.

"Your girl lives to see another day," he said, his voice lazy. He didn't care if Brianna lived or died, so he didn't care too much if the politician this orb already belonged to ever got his due. "I'm sure she'll be very grateful."

"I'm sure Senator Wilman will be too," I said.

"Take it to him," Michael ordered.

What was I, a fucking cherub delivering messages now? But I had to stay on his good side for now, so I gritted my teeth. "On my way."

I headed for the nicest part of the human side. They'd tried to make it look like Paradise 12, with marble on the finest houses and flowering trees planted everywhere.

It looked pretty for Earth.

It looked pretty shabby compared to Paradise 12, though.

I landed and dropped the Grace off at the Senator's mansion. The angel who took it from me was brusque and unsmiling, and behind him I glimpsed the red-eyed wife and a couple of kids. I wondered what it was. Cancer, maybe? We probably could've cured cancer for the humans with something besides Grace, but honestly, motivation was pretty low.

Don't worry, guys. You'll get your daddy back... And the angels will have one more politician in their pocket for the rest of his life.

I walked back out into the sunshine. I should fly back to Paradise 12 and the prison and make sure no one had forgotten that Brianna was now merely imprisoned for resisting arrest and theft instead of trafficking angelic items. She'd been bound for the torturer's pit—and the death that came with it—if I couldn't find the Grace. Illegally selling magic from angels wasn't something quickly forgiven.

I called Terrance instead. "Can you check on my special project? Make sure she's safe?"

He scoffed. "What're you going to do with that girl?"

"Recruit her to the side of all that's light and good, of course," I said, and he laughed at me, that cynical bastard.

I walked back through Halftown instead of flying. Gemma didn't need the kind of attention that came from angelic visitors. As I walked, I kept thinking about the pair of demon's blades. If Nephilim made a habit of killing angels, things were going to get ugly in Halftown. Worse still, if some Nephilim were working for the demons, it might mean the tide of war turning in their favor.

If Nephilim turned on the angels, then humanity was fucked. That was more than I could fix.

I reached the street Brianna had given me when I'd made her talk today. After the heist, I'd come back looking for her... And so had plenty of other angels. They didn't know who had done it, so they didn't know who they were looking for, but I did. Killing an angel wasn't something Nephilim got away with. But she'd disappeared from her old place without a trace. Somehow, she'd hidden away for years without us being able to find her. And fuck if I hadn't looked— more often than I wanted to admit.

I knocked on the door of Gemma and Brianna's place, not that

Brianna was ever coming back. Had she realized that yet? I kept myself on alert, fully expecting it to be a lie. There was no way she'd lived on this shitty little street that looked like every other street in Halftown all this time, hidden right out in the open, under my nose. How had she managed to keep from being detected?

It took a minute before I heard a hand press against the other side of the door.

"Who is it?" Gemma's voice called, still low and sweet like I remembered. She'd always been tender inside and out, unlike Brianna, who cloaked her vulnerable side with insolence.

So, she'd told the truth. Not that I'd given her much choice.

"It's Noah."

Would she open the door? And if she did, was it because she knew I could break it down and no one would stop me, or was it because she actually wanted to open the door? I was always curious what ran through Gemma's brain. She was so different from Brianna.

The door swung open. Gemma looked haggard, her eyes marked with dark circles, and when she smiled, her grin looked too big in her narrow face.

"You've lost too much weight," I said.

"Hello to you, too, Noah."

I strode past her into the house before she could invite me in. When she threw her arms around my neck, I shied away, almost expecting an attack.

She grinned. "Still scared of hugs, huh?"

"Hi, Gemma." I gave in and hugged her back. I could never resist the girl.

It was funny, I was an asshole to Brianna—even when we were together, to be honest—but Gemma had been like my little sister. Things between us had been easy and comfortable, and we'd been closer friends than Brianna realized. She'd acted like I wouldn't care about Gemma's fate at all. I hadn't even realized how much tension I felt coming here until I was face to face with Gemma.

"You sure you aren't going to try to murder me for disappearing and never coming back?" I side-eyed her as I pulled away.

"Brianna probably has any murdering that needs to be done under control." Gemma collapsed onto the flimsy couch. "Can I get you tea or... water?"

"No, thanks." I sat on the straight back chair opposite her, the coffee table between us. I glanced through the open door to Gemma's room, where the covers were rumpled on her bed. Gemma was the neat freak of the two. She'd been in bed, either asleep or just exhausted.

I leaned forward, my elbows braced on my knees, debating what to say next.

"Where is Brianna?" Gemma asked, chewing at her lip.

I shrugged.

"I know that's why you're here, Noah," she said.

"I should've been here for you the whole time."

"I'm betting you had a reason to stay away."

Leave it to Gemma to believe I did. I was pretty sure Brianna had just pegged my disappearance up to me being an asshole. But then, she certainly had her reasons to think I was one. She had more reasons after today.

"Maybe you've always bet a little too hard on the people around you being decent," I said to Gemma.

"Well, my instincts haven't steered me wrong yet. You're here now, aren't you?" She smiled at me, although there was something wistful in it. "And besides, you're not exactly *people*."

"I guess I'm not," I admitted, then sighed. I always had a scheme, but when I was face-to-face with Gemma, suddenly Brianna's situation seemed inescapable, even with the groundwork I'd been laying. "Brianna's in prison. Paradise 12."

Gemma's face paled.

"I've got a plan," I said. "Probably a stupid plan."

"You're looking out for her?" Gemma's voice was a little too eager. She needed to believe that.

I felt a mirthless smile twist my lips, given the brutal scene that had played out between us this morning. "I'm not sure Brianna would think so. But she's alive, despite the stupid stunt she pulled."

I explained what happened. Gemma deserved to know Brianna wasn't coming home. And Brianna deserved for Gemma to know how hard she had tried to protect her.

"Are you going to find a way for her to be pardoned?" Gemma asked, wiping away a tear. She tried to smile through her tears, and something in my chest squeezed. She had far too much faith in me.

"That's a real long shot, Gem," I said. "Just a fantasy, really."

"You've been thinking about it?"

I shrugged.

On the table between us were sad little things she and Brianna had fixed up to make the place feel homey. A candle with a blackened wick, almost burned all the way down, sat on a stack of hardback books. A pair of mason jars held sand and shells. It reminded me of how the humans had attempted to make things look like Paradise 12.

Except that the rich's attempt to dress up their part of the planet like Paradise 12 made me feel scornful, and Gemma's attempt made me feel something far more complicated, something I didn't like very much.

"Those are the shells you brought back for me," she said, following my gaze. "Remember?"

"I remember." And now I would remember how Brianna and I had climbed up the rocks, sand clinging to our feet, before she whispered that she loved me. That moment, with the girl I loved looking up at me, her black hair tossed by the clean, salt-scented breeze, and the ocean in all its majesty stretched in front of us, I'd been able to believe there could be a future for us all.

"That was a long time ago," I added.

"Doesn't feel that long ago to me," Gemma murmured.

None of the others had known that when I brought Gemma home those shells, it had been, more than anything, an excuse to go into her room, to heal her. It always left me drained, giving her that much of my Grace. I'd stumbled into Brianna's bed afterward and slept a deep, dreamless sleep.

I couldn't give Gemma the Grace that Brianna had stolen. But I could give her enough of mine for her to fight on.

"Come on, Gemma," I said, standing from the chair and offering her my hand. "Time to get some rest. You'll feel better in the morning."

She shook her head. "I can't let you do that."

"Don't be stupid," I said, and my harsh voice made her smile, strangely enough.

"I have faith in you, Noah," she said as she put her hand in mine. She was too light, bird-boned and fragile, when I pulled her to her feet.

"You shouldn't," I said as I walked her back to her room.

"Can't stop me," she whispered, leaning her head against my shoulder.

When she reached the bed, she all but collapsed into it. I pulled the covers up and sat beside her, resting my hand lightly on the side of her face. She smiled at me before her skin was suffused with a golden glow. A tugging sensation that bordered on pain flooded my nerves as the Grace slipped into her.

"Can you give a message to Brianna?" she whispered. She already sounded as if she were on the verge of sleep.

"Maybe."

She told me what she wanted to tell Brianna.

"Not too much," she added, trying to push my hand away, but she was too weak to break the bond between us. Her fingers wrapped my wrist feebly; golden veins stood out across my forearms. "You'll hurt yourself."

"Don't worry, I deserve it," I said lightly, thinking of Brianna's face beaded with sweat, her teeth clenched as she faced Uriel's blade.

Gemma's face clouded, and before she could argue with me, I added, "And you deserve it, Nephilim."

When I took my hand back, her face lolled to one side as the golden glow faded. She'd already fallen into a deep, restorative sleep.

I stumbled across the room, unsteady on my feet, and left her behind. I made sure I locked the door behind me, then reeled down the hall, feeling sick after giving her so much of my Grace.

I have faith in you, Noah.

Brianna was the most badass girl I'd ever met, but it was always our tender-hearted little sister who seemed to fuck with my head.

CHAPTER SIXTEEN

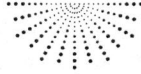

B*rianna*

"WHAT THE FUCK ARE YOU DOING?" Beckett demanded as we walked into dinner.

"The same thing as you," I said. "Going to eat after working my ass off all day."

"Except I'm not making eyes at a fucking demon."

"What?" I asked, my head jerking around toward him. "I wasn't making eyes at him."

Rhyland grinned. "So, it was him."

"No," I said sourly. "It wasn't anyone, because eyes weren't being made."

"I think we need to have a little talk," Beckett growled at me, taking my elbow.

"What, am I not allowed to eat until you say so?" I asked, pulling away. "Last time I heard, we were all prisoners. The only person who gets to order me around in here is Noah."

"It's your funeral," Beckett snapped, turning away and proceeding to ignore me as the line inched forward.

"You know, at first I figured you two were in on it together," Rhyland said casually. "You were always so tight. But he lost his shit when you disappeared and even the angels couldn't find you." He laughed like it brought him great joy to remember that.

"He thought *we* were in on it with you," Beckett muttered. "That we'd figured out his secret."

"You guys didn't know he was an angel, either?" I asked, my gaze moving back and forth between my former friends.

"Fuck, no," Beckett said. "You think we'd voluntarily hang out with one of the assholes responsible for this place?"

I nodded, swallowing hard. I didn't know how much I'd wanted that answer, how much I'd needed it, until he said it. It was so hard to know who to trust in here, so exhausting to always have to watch my back. Knowing that I hadn't been the only one duped, that Noah had lied to us all, made me feel just a little bit better. And it made me feel for the twins. They must be thinking the same thing about me—that I had known all along, that I had tricked them and made fools of them.

"I didn't know, either," I said softly. "I swear to you both. I didn't know until he caught me and brought me here."

Beckett searched my eyes as if trying to decide whether to trust me. He'd always been slower to open up and trust, and I knew better than to think my words would be all he needed. But they might be enough to make him give me another chance, the chance to prove myself.

"You didn't know you were fucking an angel," Rhyland said, shaking his head. "I figured he'd have a golden dick or something."

We all chuckled, and that broke the tension in the air as we moved forward through the line to get our food. When I stepped out of line, Anna and her posse were standing there as if they'd been waiting for me.

"I heard you got all marked up the other day," Anna said, smirking at me. "Too bad they didn't make you gouge your ugly eyes out."

Shade stepped up behind them, and our eyes met. I gave my head the slightest shake. I didn't need him stepping in. I could handle these bitches.

"I'm out of practice," I said, picking up my spoon and waving it lazily at the bitch squad. "Maybe if I gouge out all your eyes, it'll jog my memory."

"Hold my tray," Anna said, shoving her food at Samarah. "This bitch needs to learn when to keep her mouth shut."

I dropped my tray as she came at me, but Shade jumped forward to catch it, grabbing Anna around the waist with his other arm. Strong arms grabbed me from behind, too, pulling me out of Anna's reach.

"Whoa, there," Rhyland said, chuckling. "You'll get your chance to put her in her place. Fighting in the mess hall means we all get sent back to our cells, and no one gets to eat. Trust me, you don't want to be the cause of that."

Adrenaline was still pumping through me, and I pulled out of his grasp, my fists still raised and ready for the fight. But whatever Shade had said to Anna must have been a lot more menacing than Rhyland's words, because her face had gone the color of bad milk, and her hands shook so hard her utensils rattled as she took her tray back from Samarah.

Shade handed me my tray with a grin. "How's the arm?" he murmured, his voice low and sultry, like we shared some kind of dirty little secret.

"Fine, thanks," I said, not sure I liked what his sexy drawl did to my body. It seemed to remember the intimacy of our shared trauma the same way he did. Which was not how I needed to remember it at all.

"Can I see?" Shade asked, his black eyes lingering on mine.

"You heard her," Beckett gritted out, cutting between us. "She's fine."

"Alright," Shade said with a lazy grin. "Guess the fun's over now that you're here."

He turned and loped off. Beckett stormed over to an empty table and sat down without a second glance at us. Rhyland and I joined him at a slower pace.

"So," Rhyland said. "Wanna tell us again about how you weren't making eyes at that demon?"

"He's a friend," I said.

"Demons aren't our friends," Beckett muttered, attacking his food like he was picturing my face as he did it.

"Well, the angels made us both slice ourselves open, and he was nice enough to give me stitches," I said. "Which no one else could be bothered to do, I might add. He didn't have to do that, and I appreciate it. Now we're friends."

"And why do you think he gave you stitches?" Rhyland asked. "You think it was because he really wants to be your friend? Come on, Brianna. You're smarter than that."

"I don't know what he wants," I said. "But that's all we are."

"You know what he wants," Beckett snapped. "He wants to put his dick in you."

"Well, that doesn't mean he gets to," I said. "Just because every girl who wants to fuck you gets her wish fulfilled, that doesn't mean it works that way for everyone."

Rhyland laughed so hard he nearly choked on his water.

"He's a *demon*," Beckett said with a withering glare.

I shrugged. "Maybe you should think about how brainwashed you are before you go calling anyone the enemy. Shade's in here with us. He's not the one torturing us and holding us prisoner."

"No, but they're the reason we're here," Beckett said. "If it weren't for the demons trying to take over Earth, the angels wouldn't need us for their army."

"True," I said. "Our kind and his kind have been murdering each other for a hundred years, but that doesn't mean he's evil. That's how wars work. If the angels would fight their own battles, we wouldn't even be involved. We're only here because they created us to fight their wars for them."

"That's not the reason he doesn't want you talking to Shade," Rhyland said with a grin.

"Fuck off," Beckett growled at his brother.

Rhyland laughed and shook his head, but he didn't elaborate. After we dumped our trays, we headed back to our cells for the night. On the way, Rhyland threw an arm around my shoulder. "So, about that kiss the other day... How 'bout you and me pick back up where we left off?"

I shook my head, though I couldn't deny that it felt nice having him so close. It had been a long time since I'd had any kind of physical pleasure—since the night before the heist, to be exact. Feeling Rhyland's warm, muscular body pressed up against mine was doing funny things to me.

"Just tell me this," Rhyland said, his voice dropping to a murmur as we approached our cells. "If you'd known Noah was an angel, would you still have picked him?"

"What do you mean?" I asked, drawing back.

We slowed, not overly eager to reach our cells. I expected Beckett to break off from us, too proud to admit he wanted to hear the answer to Rhyland's question. But he lingered with us. I found my heart beating a little faster as I looked from one brother to the other.

"I always thought we would've made a better match," Rhyland said with a sly smile. "I know you had the hots for us both."

Before I could deny it, I felt color rising to my cheeks. I'd never dreamed of cheating on Noah, but there had always been a fun amount of attraction between me and the twins, enough to make innocent flirting fun. I'd always thought it was innocent, anyway.

"Well, I guess this is goodnight," I said, ducking into my cell. I never thought I'd be so relieved to be in a jail cell. But then Rhyland's grinning face appeared between the bars. Because lucky me, I was in the cell next to the twins. There was no escaping them.

"You never answered my question," he said.

"I don't remember a question," I said. "As I recall, you were gloating."

"He asked if you would have chosen us if you'd known Noah was an angel," Beckett said from the shadows of his bed.

"I didn't know there was a choice to be made," I said. "Neither of you ever asked me."

There was silence for a minute as they mulled that over.

93

"Because he asked you before we could," Rhyland said. "We thought he was our friend, so we never did anything about it."

"You liked me?" I asked, not quite believing it. Beckett had kind of been a dick to me, even when we were friends. And Rhyland flirted with every girl he laid eyes on—sometimes the boys, too.

"So? You liked us," Rhyland said.

"Maybe a little," I admitted. "But what does that matter? It was a long time ago."

"It matters because Noah's not our friend anymore," Rhyland said.

"He never was our friend," Beckett growled.

"Right," Rhyland said. "We respected your choice out of loyalty to him. But if you didn't know what he was, and you don't have a thing for angels…"

"What?" I asked. "Now I'm going to be one of your girlfriends?"

"Hey, I'm just saying, we could form an alliance," Rhyland said, holding up a hand and giving me a Cheshire grin. "We can protect you. But what's in it for us?"

"Tempting as that sounds, I'm not a whore."

"Oh, I don't mean it like that," he said, his eyes skimming over my body in a way that sent a shiver of want through me. "But even if we did… I think we'd make it worth your while."

"Time to sleep," I said, rolling over onto my side. Rhyland laughed his infectious laugh behind me, but it sounded delighted, not mean, as if he knew what kind of effect he had on me and it pleased him.

I pressed my knees together, trying to ignore the sudden throb between my thighs, and closed my eyes. But I could feel them moving around in their cell, settling down to sleep, as if my body was already attuned to theirs.

There was no escaping them.

And worse, I was no longer sure I wanted to.

CHAPTER SEVENTEEN

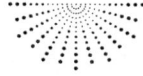

B*rianna*

I DREAMED someone trailed his fingers down my neck, my shoulder, along my side. Every place he touched raised sparks, and I smiled, not opening my eyes even as his fingers reached my hip. As he delved lower, my thighs drifted open. I couldn't get any release during the day, despite the constant sexual tension between the chaos twins and me. I was going to embrace this dream.

His hand slid between my thighs, and I let out a small moan as his fingers teased expertly against my clit. I bit my lip as desire flared into aching need. When he pulled away, my hips lifted, demanding more, and he chuckled in my ear.

Noah's chuckle.

"What are *you* thinking about?" he asked, something dismissive in his voice, which came from further away. On the other side of the room.

I scrambled up, wide awake, my dream already fading. I met his gaze evenly. "None of your business, asshole. Why are you creeping on me in my sleep?"

It was dark in the hall outside, except for the lights that ran along the floor, and Noah's big frame was shadowed as he leaned against the bars of my cell.

"It looks like I was ruining a very sweet dream," he said.

I glared at him. "Yeah, you were. I was dreaming I was fucking the twins."

I knew that blow would land, and sure enough, I could see the jealousy in his eyes, even though his lips twitched in the faintest smile.

"Sorry to interrupt." He sounded like he was mocking me, which I expected. But then his voice dropped as he added, "I know you've got more important things going on, but I wanted to tell you I saw Gemma."

My heart raced as I jumped out of bed. "You bastard. What did you do to her?"

He touched his fingers to his lips. "In here you don't want people knowing there's someone *out there* you care about."

"I don't want *you* knowing about her," I shot back, remembering Shade saying something similar.

He shrugged. "Too late. She's my friend, too."

"No, she isn't." My heart pounded imagining Noah and Gemma face-to-face. I could only imagine how Noah might use her against me. She was too tender hearted to see through him.

"Suit yourself," he said, his voice bored. "She looked well."

"Bullshit," I said. "You took the Grace I was going to give her."

It was a question, and he nodded in answer, even before he purred, "Thank you so much for your cooperation."

"Did you enjoy hurting me?" I taunted. "Is that what you get off on now? Using your power to torture inmates who can't fight back?"

He stared at me through the bars, his eyes cold. I thought he wasn't going to answer, and then he said, "No. Not particularly."

"Gemma's going to die." I closed the distance between us. Rage boiled through my blood at the sight of his coldly handsome face.

"Does that make you feel good? You won, Noah. You beat me. How does that feel?"

"Three things," he said, raising two fingers. "One, Gemma is not going to die anytime soon. She's still sick, but she's getting the best medical care Halftown has to offer, such as *that* is. So stop being so dramatic."

I frowned in confusion. Did Noah do that for her? Did he still genuinely see himself as her friend? Gemma was always easy to love. Maybe seeing her did something for Mr. Heart-of-Stone, but I couldn't let myself believe anything he was telling me. He'd never done anything but lie and manipulate me.

"Two, I'll always win, so you might as well get comfortable with losing."

I glared, absently scratching between the ugly wounds that were just beginning to heal on my arm.

He let the silence between us linger, studying me with his bright eyes. I leaned against the bars on my side, which brought us intimately close together.

"What's three?" I demanded.

"Three *was* a message from Gemma," he mused. "But I guess I forgot it, during all that time you were trying so hard to hurt my feelings."

Rage tightened my chest. There was probably no message; he was just saying whatever would rile me up. He probably hadn't even seen her. "I'm not that stupid, Noah. I'd never waste my energy trying to hurt *your feelings*. You don't have any, especially when it comes to Nephilim. We're no more than robots to you. Just something to take the blows on the battlefield so your kind don't have to."

"You're just full of wrong answers today."

"I hate you," I told him, gripping the bars, the words boiling out of me. "You're the cruelest, most self-centered piece of shit I've ever met. I can't believe you ever fooled me into giving a fuck about you."

He nodded, listening with a blank face, as if nothing I said meant anything to him. "You're not telling me anything you didn't tell me in that cell."

"I'm going to fucking kill you, Noah," I warned him.

He reached between the bars and grabbed my chin between his fingers, pulling me close to him. His fingers were a relentless cruel grip. I reached between the bars, trying to get my hands around his throat.

"Watch what you say," he whispered. "If the warden heard you, he'd have you flogged for threatening an angel. I'm not the worst enemy you have in here, sweetheart."

"You're wrong," I whispered. "Nothing he could do would hurt worse than what you've already done."

My hand squeezed around his throat, but he just smiled at me, a familiar Noah smile that used to make my heart do flip-flops, before he caught my wrist in his crushing grip. He pulled my hand away from him and then yanked my wrist, forcing my face against the bars as he extended my arm. I gritted my teeth as he examined the wounds and the stitches.

"Someone's got neat work," he commented. "Who did this? You? Or the doctor?"

"Fuck you," I whispered, knowing he was right, that in public I should be careful what I said to an angel. "I'm not giving you one more thing to use against me."

"I already have everything I need to use against you, babe," he said, giving me a wink as the sardonic word rolls off his tongue. *Babe* sounded ridiculous in the mouth of an angel. "But I could use someone with these kinds of skills on my team. I'd like to thank them for patching you up."

His team? What the hell was he talking about? And why the hell did he care if I was patched up nicely when he was the one who had sadistically forced me to slice myself open to begin with? A sense of dread rippled through me. He always had a scheme, and I had a feeling his next one involved me.

He released my arm, and I stumbled back a step before I caught myself. He was already turning to go, but he stopped and turned back, his face blank.

"Gemma said thank you," he said. "For trying. She said you're the sister she never had, and she loves you."

His words each hit like a brick. I didn't know what to make of those sweet words, delivered in Noah's cold, heartless voice.

He turned and sauntered down the cell block. My chest was tight as I watched him go. I didn't know what to make of anything Noah had said about Gemma. If I believed him, that she was getting the best medical care, it would give me a huge sense of relief. But I didn't know if I could trust him even with this.

"Fucking the twins, huh?" Rhyland said, chuckling.

Damn. They'd heard that.

"Go back to sleep, Rhy," I warned him, but even as I stumbled into my bed, I knew I wouldn't fall back asleep.

It didn't matter anyway, because a few minutes later, the alarm sounded, and the lights blazed on—blindingly bright and painful, the way they always woke us up.

"Welcome to another beautiful morning in Paradise," Rhyland sing-songed to no one.

Beckett grunted. "Please shut up."

That day, I couldn't shake the uneasiness that wormed its way through my body. There was something about my encounter with Noah that had left me shaken, and it wasn't just that he'd spoken of Gemma. On top of worrying about her, now I had to protect Shade from Noah now, too. I couldn't shake the feeling that I was missing something else in our conversation, something important.

Maybe Beckett and Rhyland remembered my bad moods, because even though the three of us ate our meals together and they shadowed me relentlessly, they didn't provoke me today. As we were leaving the training yard, though, a guard stepped to block my way. "You're to see the warden."

Beckett and Rhyland exchanged a glance.

"What'd you do?" Beckett muttered.

This probably had to do with Noah, but I didn't want to reveal I had any kind of past with him in front of the guard. I kept all my secrets to myself in here.

"Now," the guard warned, holding up a pair of manacles.

"Now," I agreed, flashing him a sweet smile as I held my wrists out. He clipped the manacles around my wrists, as if I were going to take the warden hostage and fight my way out of here. Well, maybe that wasn't an entirely bad idea. I didn't know what Noah had planned for me, given that he'd gone through the trouble of coming to visit me this morning, but I'd imagined I'd just be left to rot here until I died.

"See you boys later," I told Rhyland and Beckett before the guard took me away, but I could see the worry on their faces, and it made me nervous.

Just when I thought I knew what was coming next in this place, what our routine was, and that there was no reason for Noah to mess with me anymore, things shifted again. I'd given him the Grace. What more could he want?

It was strange to have a different guard walk me through the prison. It had always been Noah who led me through, his hand wrapped on the nape of my neck, firm and possessive, as if he still thought he owned some part of me. This guard didn't touch me except to shove me roughly forward when I saw Shade in the hall and hesitated.

Shade's gaze sharpened, as if he could tell I was in trouble. "Watch out," he mouthed at me.

It didn't matter that he didn't even speak the words out loud. The guard, as we drew even with Shade, yanked his baton out and slammed it into Shade's gut.

Shade doubled over, falling to his knees on the hard grating of the floor. I jumped toward him, and the guard pushed me away, so hard that I stumbled and almost fell without being able to catch myself.

Shade was on his feet in a flash, faster than any human could move, grabbing my arm to steady me.

"Don't speak in my presence, demon scum," the guard said in a warning voice.

Shade raised his hands in a gesture of surrender, even though his eyes were livid with fury.

Again, I wondered if the Nephilim were on the right side of this war.

CHAPTER EIGHTEEN

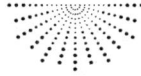

B*rianna*

"BRIANNA," the warden said, giving me a smile that made my skin crawl as he gestured for me to enter his office. If I'd expected something grim because we were in a prison, I should have known better. We'd climbed a never-ending set of winding stairs to reach his office, which sat perched in what could only be described as a luxury guard tower. It loomed over the prison, and all four walls were made of glass, so he could spy on the prisoners below any time he pleased. As if he couldn't monitor us on cameras, he had to sit over us like a king in a throne room. I hated the bastard on sight.

"Warden," I said with a curt nod.

"Have a seat," he said, gesturing to the gilded chair opposite his expansive glass desk.

Knowing I should pick my battles, I sat. As he circled his desk, I ran my fingers along the gold edges of my chair. I wondered how much this would get on the black market. How many days a Nephilim in Halftown could eat, or how much medicine Gemma could get, for the sale of a chair that the warden let prisoners sit in—when they had the privilege of visiting him.

The warden sat opposite me, tenting his hands on the desk in front of him and staring at me with his sharp, blue eyes. I studied him back, slouching in the chair and refusing to quake under what he probably thought was an intimidating gaze. His blond hair was combed back to reveal a widow's peak, and his face was all angles and corners. I supposed he was handsome, if you could get past the cold, calculating look in his eyes, like a snake about to strike.

"As you know, I'm Warden Jacob," he started. "I've been watching you since you arrived, Brianna."

"Okay," I said slowly.

"Very interesting choice of companions," he mused.

"Not that interesting," I said with a shrug. I may have looked like an indolent, uncooperative brat, but I was ready for whatever he was working up to. He must have a reason for calling me in instead of leaving me to Noah's sadistic tortures. Surely he didn't care that much that I'd taken help from a demon. If they cared that much about keeping us separate, they wouldn't have thrown us all in prison together.

"Do you realize," Jacob said slowly, tapping his index fingers together as he stared at me over the tent of his fingers, "How difficult it is for a prisoner—any prisoner—to get close to the boys you've chosen as friends?"

So it wasn't about Shade at all. It was about the chaos twins.

"I'm sure it's not too hard," I said with a smirk. "They'll be best friends with anyone with a vagina for a few days, at least."

"But you're not just anyone, are you, Brianna?" he asked, his voice a twisting snake of deceit. He was trying to trap me. I just didn't know what he wanted me to reveal yet. I could wait him out.

"I'm not just anyone," I agreed. "I'm someone with a vagina."

"But you're more than that to them, aren't you?" he asked, twirling his finger in the air. A holographic screen popped up, and he slid his finger through the lines of gold and blue, scrolling for something. He continued talking, his voice a musing drawl, as if he were just as unconcerned with this visit as I was pretending to be. I didn't know where this game of cat and mouse was going, but I was liking it less every second.

"You see, a few years back, when the twins arrived here, there was a crime in the Halftown they lived in," he says. "In fact, they were involved in it. They claimed to have acted alone. Even making Ryland disfigure his own brother's face couldn't convince him to say otherwise."

Suddenly, my hands balled into fists, and a sick sensation washed through my stomach. This asshole hadn't just made Beckett hurt himself. That would be bad enough. I'd still want to rip his head off for that. But no, he'd gone one step further. He'd forced Rhyland to hurt his own brother—his own twin—or turn me in. And the really fucked up part was, they hadn't. Rhyland had hurt his brother to protect me. And Beckett had taken the pain rather than rat me out to the angels.

Beckett had gotten that scar protecting me. Rhyland had given it for the same reason. Beckett might claim to hate me, but damn. He'd endured that pain instead of squealing, even though he thought I'd sent the angels after them. Suddenly, I wanted nothing but to get out of there and go talk to the twins. I owed them my life—and probably Gemma's, too.

Warden Jacob was watching me, waiting for me to react. I'd already shown too much, though. He wasn't getting anything else from me. They'd saved my life, and I sure as hell wasn't going to take that for granted.

"You're angry that I hurt your friends," the warden said.

"Yeah, just like I'm pissed that you hurt me, and I'd be pissed if you tortured anyone else in here," I said. "You're a bunch of sadistic psychopaths."

"But that's not the only reason, is it, Brianna?" he purred. "You see, they weren't the only people we could ask about that night. There were several witnesses who reported seeing a girl fleeing the scene. A girl who fits your description."

I snorted. "Oh, please. I'm a world-class thief. Do you really think I'd pull a heist without a disguise?"

The warden's eyebrow twitched. It was the smallest tic, an involuntary one he probably didn't even know he'd shown, but I could tell I'd annoyed him.

"Brianna," he said, recovering himself smoothly. "We have your academy records. Records for all three of you. We know you were friends before coming here."

Damn it. Why hadn't I seen that coming?

"So?"

"So, we have every reason to believe that you're the one who disappeared the night of the murder. In fact, we all but know it. The only thing we don't know is how you managed to hide from us for so long. Of course we traced you back to your place in Halftown the very morning after the twins were arrested, but you were nowhere to be found. How did you manage to stay hidden for two whole years, Brianna?"

I shrugged. "I moved. That's not a crime. And I wasn't there the night the twins were arrested, or I'd have been arrested with them."

We had moved—the same night as the heist. When the guys hadn't shown up at the rendezvous point, Gemma and I had gone home, thinking the twins and Noah had scattered when things went wrong, headed back to their own houses to hunker down until the angels left. I'd dragged Gemma with me and run, staying in abandoned buildings for the next few days. When I'd gone back a few days later to gather a few things from our home, I'd seen the angels swarming the streets. That's when I'd known something had gone really wrong. I hadn't realized the angel was dead until then.

"Tell me," the warden said, leaning forward. "How could a single Nephilim girl kill an angel?"

"She couldn't," I said. "No Nephilim can kill an angel."

They were practically invincible. When the angel came at me, I'd panicked, and a rush of hot adrenaline and power coursed through me when I thought he was about to rip my head off. But that happened when you thought you were about to die. I'd thrown him off and run. I hadn't even used a weapon.

What I didn't know was who had really killed him.

The twins hadn't been near him. I didn't know what he was at the time, but looking back, the killer had to have been Noah. He was the only one strong enough to kill an angel.

But if he'd been on their side all along, why would he kill one of them?

Obviously his cover had been blown that night, and he'd come back to Paradise 12 to live in angelic luxury for the next three years, letting them believe that I was the killer. After all, they couldn't find me, so I was an easy target. But that didn't really make sense, either, since no one would believe that I'd done it alone. So who *had* killed the angel?

None of it made sense.

"Well, this is a disappointment," the warden said after a long moment of studying me. "Here I thought the last piece of the puzzle had been found after all this time. That you might be the one to give us what we want."

"I gave you the Grace," I said. "That's all I have."

"I don't think so," Warden Jacob said. "I think you have the truth."

"The truth is, I didn't kill that angel, and I don't know who did."

"I think you do," Jacob said, his piercing gaze knifing into mine. "I think we both do."

"Okay, I'll play," I said, crossing my arms over my chest. "How, exactly, do you think I killed a full-blooded angel? I'm a Nephilim."

"With help," he said, a cruel smile twisting his lips.

"Well, I didn't," I said.

"Very well," he said with a shrug. "I've been waiting for two years to send your little friends off to the front. Your old friend Noah has a soft spot for those cretins, wanted to keep them around until we could prove for sure they did it. But now I see that was a waste of time. They're murderers, and they deserve to die at the front."

Noah had been protecting the twins? A hollow opened up in my chest at the thought, but I told myself he must have had some twisted reason.

"What? No!" I said, sitting up straight. "They're innocent!"

It was a strange word to apply to the twins, but they hadn't killed that angel.

"Well, if you're not going to clear their names and confess, then they must have been in on it," the warden said. "So, what's it going to be, Brianna? Did you somehow kill that angel, and if you did, how? If you didn't do it alone, then surely all three of you did it. That's the only way I can imagine a Nephilim killing a true angel."

All three of us? Did he even know that Noah was there that night? Noah was no friend of mine, and yet I didn't want to tell this guy anything more than I had to.

"What if I did?" I asked, stalling for time. My heart was racing in my chest. Sending any of us to the front was a death sentence.

"Then you'll go to the front alone."

"And they'll be released?" I asked. "If I did it alone, then they're innocent. Right?"

"I wouldn't go so far as to use that word," the warden drawled. "They were stealing our sacred relics. They haven't exactly impressed me with their good behavior in the prison, either."

"But they won't get sent to the front?"

"Are you saying you killed that angel alone?"

I swallowed hard, gripping the gilded arms of the chair. "Yes."

He stared at me a long moment, his blue eyes so cold they could make a demon shiver. "Funny. They said the same thing."

"Great. We all agree. You can send me to the front and let them go."

"No," he said slowly, leaning back in his chair. "They said they acted alone, too. Which means you're all trying to protect each other. Just as I thought, you have an emotional connection with them."

A slow smile spread over his face at the idea. "How intriguing. I didn't think anyone could break through their shells."

Fuck. This asshole had me trapped, and there was nothing I could do to get out of it. Even confessing hadn't gotten any of us out of here.

"What do you want?" I growled.

"I want to know how you killed an angel," he said.

"I can't tell you that, because I didn't kill him," I said, exasperated that we seemed to be talking in circles.

"Then the twins killed him. You've just been lying to me for your own amusement."

"No," I said sharply.

"Then who killed him, Brianna?" Jacob asked, a vicious edge to his voice. "Because an angel was murdered, and someone has to pay for it. There is no statute of limitations when you hurt one of our own."

"Fine," I said, taking a deep breath. "It was me. I killed him."

"How?" he asked, his voice slow and deliberate.

I wracked my brain, trying to think of some way to kill an angel. "With... The relics," I said, making shit up as I went. "I got out one of the relics, and I bashed him with it, and he died. It must have been some kind of magic—I didn't expect it. It was an accident. And then I freaked out and ran away so you couldn't find me."

At least now I knew that Noah cared about Gemma, that he'd go back and tell her what had happened to me. He might even help her. And even if he didn't, I was never getting out of here either way. I'd never be able to help her again. I might as well help the twins. After all, they'd spent two years in this hell when I'd been free. Maybe it was my turn to pay for my part in that night's disaster.

"Why would I believe you, when you and your friends each tried to take responsibility?"

I leaned forward. "You used Uriel's blade on both of them, didn't you? I can't imagine you would have a toy like that at your disposal and not use it on them."

His lips parted in a faint smile. I had him. But fuck, they'd tortured Rhyland and Beckett for answers they didn't have, that they couldn't give. And somehow, they still didn't entirely believe them, even though the blades forced the truth.

"They didn't see me do it," I said. "They didn't know for sure who killed that angel. That's why they couldn't tell you, even under torture."

Just thinking of that gleaming blade shining under the fluorescent lights as it pressed against my skin made fear twist through my guts. I flashed him my sweetest smile, even though I knew it didn't reach my eyes. "I'm happy to play that game, though. I killed that angel—and I can prove it."

"Very well," the warden said, seemingly satisfied with my confession at last. "Your friends stole from us. They'll remain here. But you, my little halfling, are a murderer of angels. You will go to the front to die."

CHAPTER NINETEEN

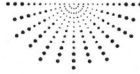

B *rianna*

A STRANGE, giddy sense took over as the guard walked me back. It was surreal—the mystery of who had killed the angel, the warden's pronouncement.

Few survived the front, and no one survived it if they were sent there indefinitely. The warden had just sentenced me to death.

There was an appropriate reaction to that news, and it was not the reaction I was having.

When I reached the hall where I lived now, it seemed empty at first. Right. It was lunch time. I was about to miss another meal. I didn't care right now.

Beckett was laying on my bed, so still that I had missed him at first. His gaze was fixed on the ceiling, his arms tucked under his head.

"Making yourself comfortable?" I asked.

He smirked in response.

"Why are you in my bed, Rhy?"

He glanced at me, then gave me a wink that felt cursory. "The question is why aren't I always, Bri?"

"I had a long talk with the warden," I said.

"I figured as much."

"You were waiting here to see how I might have betrayed you?" My voice came out tart. I still resented how they'd taken to the idea.

And yet...they had protected me.

"I was waiting here to see what the warden wanted with my property. I don't like anyone else playing with my toys."

I reached the side of my own bed and straddled him quickly. He jerked up in surprise, staring at me, perplexed as my knees settled on either side of his hips.

"Let me see that scar." I ran my fingers through his hair, brushing it back from his forehead.

His eyes weren't cold anymore—they were dark and dangerous and very, very alive. "What the hell do you think you're doing?"

"The warden told me that he tried to find out who killed the angel the night everything went to hell," I said. "He told me that he used you and Rhyland to hurt each other."

His eyes met mine evenly. "Don't take that as a sign of my undying affection, Brianna. I didn't know the answer. I didn't see you do it."

"You knew who else was there that night."

He just stared at me, the air between us charged. He couldn't even admit to what he'd done for me.

His hands gripped my hips. "What do you want from me?"

"I want you to admit that you were trying to protect me," I said, my voice coming out teasing, even though I meant it.

They'd tried to protect me, and I'd tried to protect *them,* and now I was going to die for it. He could at least tell the truth.

I was always a bit on the reckless side, but tonight I felt more reckless than I ever had before.

"Sorry," he drawled. "Not happening."

"You're a liar, Beckett," I said, trailing my fingers from his forehead down his scarred cheek to that chiseled jaw. "So tough on the outside, and yet not tough enough to admit who you really are…"

He grabbed my wrists, his hands painfully tight, but then he just stared up at me. He didn't even move my hand from his face.

"Just because I protected you doesn't mean you deserved it," he growled.

I almost laughed. He was so damned stubborn. He still gripped my wrists, so I leaned forward into his touch instead of pulling away, my elbows resting on his hard pecs. His hard cock pressed against my thigh.

"Does it turn you on when I boss you around?" I teased him.

"Does it turn you on when I contemplate strangling you?"

"Well, Noah could tell you that I like a little of that," I purred, just to make him miserable. His eyes went feral at the name. "But despite your best efforts, I know you'd never really hurt me, Beckett."

"If I were you—"

I cut him off, pressing my lips against his. Whatever wicked lie he was about to tell me died on his lips. For a second, his mouth resisted mine, then his lips parted against mine and he kissed me back.

His bruising grip finally left my wrists. One hand threaded through my hair, holding my face against his. He deepened the kiss, nudging my lips open with his tongue. As our tongues slid together, I felt his heart hammering in his chest beneath my hands.

For all I'd said any girl could be Beckett's best friend for an hour, I had to wonder if there was something different between us. When I felt the way his body responded to mine, and when I thought about what he and Rhyland had endured for me, I knew I'd always meant more to him than he'd let on.

His hands gripped my back, the curve of my ass, sweeping over my body as if he couldn't get enough of me. I pulled away from him, my long hair swaying around my shoulders as I straightened. His hands wrapped around my hips.

"What's this about, Brianna?" he asked, his voice rough—with emotion or desire, I couldn't tell. "Did you decide to take our deal?"

A mirthless smile slipped across my lips. Oh yes—their deal to protect me.

"What did you do?" he demanded, his grip tightening.

"It doesn't matter," I said. It was already done. I didn't know when they were going to pull me off to the front, but I knew I wanted to live all I could in the meantime, and until I left, I wanted these two men that I used to love. They'd always been friends, no matter how much they tried to make themselves out as villains. They'd always been mine.

Beckett curled to sit up, despite me straddling his lap, which brought our faces intimately close. He gripped my chin in his fingers, studying my eyes.

"You and I aren't doing a damn thing until you tell me the rest of your conversation with the Warden, Brianna."

"I didn't think you'd ever choose talking over fucking," I teased him. "You know we won't be alone forever…"

"I don't care about being alone," he warned. "But I do want to know what stupid thing you've done."

I held his gaze. "The warden said he's been trying to send you and Rhy to the front for years. That Noah convinced him not to."

Beckett scoffed. "I doubt that very much."

"Noah insisted you not go until there was enough proof—until the last person from the heist was caught. Now, I've been caught."

"Fuck," he muttered, running his hand through his hair as the meaning behind my words sank in, and he realized their time was up. "Rhyland… I wouldn't care for me, but Rhy…"

Of course his first thought was always for his twin brother, no matter how hard he pretended to be.

"You don't have to go," I said. "I mean, it's not like this place is a resort, but at least it's not the front."

Glittering eyes met mine, full of understanding, but he still demanded, "What did you do?"

"I confessed."

Those two words hung in the room.

"No," Beckett growled. He shook his head, "Take it back. Every-thing Rhyland and I went through to protect you—"

"So you *did* protect me," I said, an edge of triumph in my voice. "You admit it?"

He just glared.

"I can't take it back," I said with a shrug. "And I wouldn't if I could. I knew everything went to shit that night, but I didn't know what happened to the two of you. But you guys were punished for it for two years, and I'm not going to keep letting you take the fall all the way to the front."

"You're going to do what I fucking tell you," he said.

I didn't even dignify that with an answer. I'd never been the obedient type, and I sure as hell wasn't going to start now.

Instead, I gripped him through his pants. "I don't know when I'll be leaving," I said. "But before I go…"

"You're not going anywhere," he growled. "I won't let you."

I almost laughed at that. We were both prisoners. How could he protect me?

"It's my turn to protect you, the one way I can, and you can't stop me," I said as I pushed him down on the bed. My lips met his, claiming him. The two of us undressed each other in frenzied, hurried move-ments, trading kisses the whole time.

We jockeyed for position on the narrow bed until we rolled off, landing hard on the cement floor of the cell. I barely noticed as my knees slammed into the cement, my body cushioned by Beckett's underneath me. His hands were in my hair, pulling me close to him, kissing me like he couldn't get enough of me.

My hands swept down his chiseled abs, down his thighs. His cock was long and thick when I gripped him and pressed his tip against my opening. He slowly pressed into me, filling me inch by slow inch, watching my face. I bit my lip at the sensation. It had been so long, and he was so big, and despite his tough act, he frowned with concern.

He started to say something, maybe to ask if I was all right, but I didn't want him to keep acting like I was so damned fragile that he had to protect me. I wanted him. I pressed down on him, burying him in me to the hilt, until my thighs pressed against his rock hard abs. He was so big he hurt, just a little. He caught me with a hand on the back of my neck, drawing me down to him and kissing me tenderly this time. My muscles relaxed around him until the discomfort faded.

As pleasure replaced the pain, I rose up and down his shaft. His hands gripped my hips hard, helping me keep time as I rode him. Those beautiful eyes of his bled from soft green to a blazing emerald with desire. We moved faster and faster, caught up in the moment, until I couldn't help a low groan that built deep in my chest and slipped through my mouth. Beckett's lips met mine, kissing me as if that moan was delicious, his fingers tightening in my hair as he drove into me.

"God, you're so fucking tight," he growled, pushing himself into a sitting position. Wrapping his strong arm around my waist and bracing his other hand on the floor, he thrust up into me while slamming me down on him.

"Oh god," I gasped as the new position hit all the right places inside me. "I'm going to come."

"Thank fuck," Beckett said, dragging my chest to his and holding me against him, grinding his hips up against mine as his hot seed spilled into me, and my walls clenched around him as I came.

"Well, look what finally happened."

I jerked my head up, still spinning from my orgasm, to find Ryland standing outside the bars.

He let out a delighted laugh.

"How long have you been watching?" Beckett asked, although he didn't sound particularly annoyed. He kissed me again, a quick, sweet kiss, before lifting me off him and climbing to his feet. He cleaned himself up with his T-shirt, then tossed it to me. "You could have joined in."

"Did you finally accept our proposition?" Rhyland asked. "You've always been meant to be our girl, Brianna. Glad to see you've sealed the deal."

"No," Beckett scoffed. "Brianna's too stubborn for something so simple."

I rolled my eyes.

"No," Beckett said again. "We're going to have to break *our girl* out of prison, or she's as good as dead."

"Excuse me?" I asked.

Beckett gave me a cocky smile. "We're going to save your life, sweetheart."

CHAPTER TWENTY

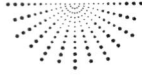

R *hyland*

WE TRAINED THE NEXT DAY, none of us talking much, though I knew we were all thinking the same thing. How the hell were we going to escape before they took Brianna?

We knew better than to discuss escape plans at dinner. But after lights-out, in the dark of our cells, before the guards made their first round, we met at the bars between our two cells. I wished I could tear them down, burn this whole fucking place to the ground, but if I could have done that, I would have done it two years ago when they brought me here and forced me to hurt my own brother. If that weren't bad enough, they made me do it on his face, where I'd have to see it for the rest of my fucking life.

I shook the thought away and pressed my knee against Brianna's, wishing I could touch more of her, like he had. But there was no use wishing in a place like this.

"Any ideas?" Brianna asked.

"We could tell him you were lying," Beckett said. "Since you were."

"No," Brianna said. "I'm not letting you go get killed."

"And we're not letting you," Beckett snapped back.

"Hate to interrupt your little lover's quarrel," I said. "But that's not really an option. He's not going to believe us any more than he did last time, when we said we acted alone."

"I'm sorry that happened," Brianna said, touching my knee. Her fingers were warm, and just like when I kissed her, one touch had my cock jerking like a horse that wanted to break his reins and run free. And what a glorious run that would be.

"It's a lot harder to plan something when we don't know when the next batch will be taken to the front," I said, trying to ignore my cock and the fact that her hand was still on my knee.

"They don't give you a calendar, or let you watch the news to see how the war's going?" Brianna said drily. We hadn't even done that shit in Halftown, let alone here. They didn't want us knowing anything that might compromise their mission. And hell, if we shipped out every Tuesday, we'd know what to expect. The effectiveness of the angels' reign of terror relied on us living in fear, never knowing what came next. Oldest trick in the book—because it fucking worked.

"Which means the sooner we get out of here, the better," Beckett said at last.

"Maybe we could hide ourselves in a shipment of something," Brianna said. "Or… When a food delivery truck comes. What if we could sneak out in one of those?"

Trust Brianna to be sneaky as fuck. She'd been a con and a thief long enough to have a few tricks up her sleeve.

"It's risky," Beckett said, scratching his chin. "They search those pretty well before they leave, and they pass through thermal scanners on their way through the gates. We could maybe get you out."

"No," she said, shaking her head. "All or none. I'm not leaving you here any longer than I already have. If I'd known you were here…"

"You didn't," Beckett said, taking her free hand through the bars and squeezing.

So, apparently fucking her had made him forgive and forget all the shit in the past. But hell, who was I kidding? If she'd picked me, if I'd been the one who fucked her, I'd be kissing her ass now, too. The ungenerous thought popped into my head that maybe if I'd been the one sent to my cell to miss lunch, she would have picked me instead. Which meant she hadn't really chosen Beckett over me. He'd just been in the right place at the right time. Lucky bastard.

"Or," I said slowly, my mind circling back to the recruits shipping out to the front. "We could all go to the front with the new recruits."

"No," Brianna said. "I can't let you do that for me."

I smirked at her. "We're not really going to the front."

I watched the realization dawning in both her and my brother. "We won't know when they're shipping out," Beckett pointed out.

"It won't matter," I said. "We just fall in with the ones being called. They gather them all at the shipping dock, load them up in a crowded truck, and ship them off. So, we'll just slip into the crowd and go with."

"And then what?" Brianna asked.

"When they stop, we make a run for it," I said. "We'll be outside the prison gates, so it won't be too hard. We'll just have to outwit a guard or two. Piece of cake."

"We don't know where they'll stop," Beckett said, always the cautious one.

"Doesn't matter," I said. "It won't be in any Paradise crawling with angels. We'll hide out for a few days in whatever wasteland we're passing through."

"Just the three of us?" Brianna asked, looking thoughtful.

"Yes," I said, before she could ask to take along her demon buddy, which I was sure she was thinking about. "The more people we take, the harder it will be. We have to keep it small. Just us."

"Okay," she said, nodding. "I think it's the best we can do for now. They won't be expecting anyone to try to go to the front by choice, so it will be easier to get out that way. Plus, the truck is already filled with people, so the thermal scanner won't see anything abnormal."

"Right," Beckett said. "It's the best way to get outside the gates. Good thinking, Rhy." He gave me a quick, tight smile.

I couldn't help smiling back, a lot bigger. I had to admit, it felt fucking good to be planning some illegal activity with Brianna again. The heists had always been a thrill for me.

True, she could rat us out, tell the warden our plan and save her own ass. He'd probably switch us out then, sending us to die and letting her stay. But if she was going to do that, why protect us in the first place?

Unless she'd been planning this all along, knowing we were suckers for her...

No. I wasn't going to let them come between us again. I knew she hadn't turned us in after the heist. It had never made sense, anyway. The angels had caught us when we'd stopped to hide. Later, they'd told us that Brianna had ratted us out, pointed them to our hiding place. But if that were true, why didn't they have her in custody, too? They weren't going to take her word for it, let her go, and then come find us—and then start interrogating us about where *she* had disappeared to. It had never made sense. And now we knew why. Because like always, the angels were full of shit.

"Yeah," Brianna said, her eyes shining with the same excitement as mine. "Thanks, Rhyland. That's a great plan."

She leaned forward, sliding her arm through the bars and pulling me into an awkward hug, with our knees pressed together and the bars separating us. But it was the best we could do until we were out of this god forsaken place. Then, I could touch her all I wanted.

Unless Beckett thought he'd have her all to himself. I decided right then that I wasn't going to let that happen. I pulled Brianna's face to mine and kissed her. At first she tensed, but then her lips responded to mine, her mouth as eager to relive our kiss as mine was. I slid a hand behind her head, burying it in her silky strands and pressing deeper into the kiss.

"I think that's enough," Beckett growled.

Brianna began to draw back, but I held her tighter, angling my face and deepening the kiss even more, slipping my tongue between her lips to taste her mouth again. She melted into me, reaching through the bars to wrap her arms around me, trying to get closer. Fuck, I wanted to be closer. I wanted to pin her to the wall and bury myself in her. God, my cock was so hard it ached for her, but these goddamn bars were holding us apart.

I heard footsteps outside, the guard coming to do his rounds. Beckett cleared his throat before reluctantly returning to his bed. He might not like it right now, but he'd realize it was for the best. He wanted me to be happy, just like I wanted him to be. And the only way we'd both be happy was if we both got Brianna. We'd shared girls before. He must have thought that because Brianna was special, he'd get her to himself. But I knew it was the opposite. Because she was special, neither of us could be greedy and selfish. We wouldn't let her come between us, and she wouldn't want to. She wanted us both. So, this was the way it was, and I was making sure he knew it.

I plunged my tongue into her mouth, taking everything I could get before the guard could tell us to go back to bed. Brianna moaned, her nails digging into my scalp as she pressed her cheeks to the bars, trying to get closer.

A loud bang sounded as the guard's club hit the metal bars, sending vibrations through the entire cell, including the bars we were straining against.

"Get back in your beds," Noah barked.

Brianna drew away, letting her wet lips linger on mine another few seconds before clambering slowly to her feet. "Yes, *Master*," she said, her tone sweet but laced with loathing as she gave Noah a one-finger salute and strolled over to her bed and flopped down.

Noah glared at me like he wanted to kill me. The feeling was mutual.

"You, too," he said, coldly.

"What'd you think would happen if you put her in the next cell over—that we wouldn't fuck her?" I asked, sauntering back to my bed. "Face it, asshole, you had your chance, and you couldn't keep her. Now she's ours, and you're out there all by yourself. Bet you're not feeling so high and mighty now."

"From what I heard, you can't keep her either," Noah said, his voice cold. "You pricks got her sent to the front."

"Oh, go away, Noah." Brianna waved him off dismissively. "I'm already going to the front to die, you don't need to annoy me to death first."

Noah didn't answer, but he stared at her, something hard and glittering in his eyes. He inhaled, his chest heaving, as if he had something he needed to say.

I raised my gaze to meet his, my glare boring into his.

He stared back at me. Whatever he had intended to say died on his lips, and he considered me before he asked, "You three are far stupider than I thought, aren't you?"

Then he turned and walked on, that baton gripped lazily in one hand. *That's right, walk away, you blessed motherfucker.* But I couldn't even hate Noah that much right now—I was too focused on Brianna, just on the other side of the bars.

I lay back on my bed, liking the sound of my claim. She was ours. Not mine, not Beckett's. *Ours.*

"You good with this, brother?" I asked quietly.

"I'm good," Beckett said. "Bri?"

"*So* good," she said from the next cell.

"So, we've got a plan," Beckett said after a long five minutes, when we'd heard Noah leave the cellblock.

"And what's the worst that can happen?" I asked. "If they catch us, they'll just put us back in the truck and ship us where we were already going. The front is a death sentence. They can't do worse than that."

CHAPTER TWENTY-ONE

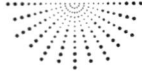

N *oah*

WHEN I WALKED into the training yard toward the end of the next day, it fell silent in ripples as people saw me and stopped. The sounds of panting and skin meeting skin in the most brutal of ways quieted. The faces that turned my way when there were no bars between us promised that, despite the fact their actions would be a death sentence, some of them were gauging their chances to kill me.

I'd brought an awful lot of Nephilim to prison.

After all, no one understood them as well as I did. I'd spent years in the brutal training academy, listening to their drunken existential crises, their frustration that they fit nowhere—neither with the humans they didn't respect nor the angels they despised.

I could've told them that no one fits in anywhere.

"Still got eyes on them?" Isham asked, tapping his baton absently against his leg as he watched the prisoners. Someone glared at me, a glare that promised death, but I didn't spare him a second glance. I followed Isham's gaze to where Rhyland and Beckett stood—with Brianna, of course—right before the instructors started yelling that if they didn't want to fight, they could just accept being beaten.

I thought there were more meaningful training methods we could employ beside having them brutalize each other daily, but I was barely hanging onto what power I had here. I'd overextended myself with the warden, trying to keep Rhyland and Beckett from the front. But it would all be worth it in the end.

I shook my head in frustration. "We'll see if my team ever happens."

"Good ideas die in bureaucracy," Isham agreed.

"I came to take one of them for interrogation," I said.

"I'll call her over."

I side-eyed him but didn't argue. Isham knew me well, but it still bothered me that anyone saw the soft spot I had for Brianna. I hid it so well from her. Why couldn't I hide it from him?

"You," he said, tapping my chest lightly with the baton before pointing to the mass of training Nephilim, "Shouldn't go over *there*. It might be too tempting."

I shrugged. Being mobbed by the prisoners was a constant danger. When I first came here and tended to be too soft, I'd checked on an injured Nephilim, let down my guard, only to discover he was bait for the half-dozen that jumped me. I'd lost my baton and had to fight them hand-to-hand. That had been a bad day—for me and for them.

But here, where there were so many guards, they'd have to be very stupid indeed.

Isham brought Brianna out of the training line. Her eyes narrowed when she saw me, her pace slowing, and Isham shoved her forward. She stumbled and, in the second before she caught herself, my chest tightened with rage. I wanted to punch Isham for laying his hands on her.

But it was my eyes she met with pure fury. She didn't spare him a glance.

"Can't stay away, Noah?" she asked, her voice glib.

"How could I, when you're so charming?" I swept my arm toward the doors out of the training yard.

She walked ahead of me, casting one wary, searching glance back over her shoulder, probably looking for Beckett and Rhyland. A fresh wave of raw jealousy washed over me.

"What's your excuse for spending time with me now?" she asked.

"I heard all about your little chat with the warden," I said.

Her pace slowed as she tried to walk by my side, as if we were equals, which would not go unnoticed. I grabbed the back of her neck, pushing her ahead of me.

Tension rippled through her shoulders and her chin rose.

"You could come to the front with me, Noah," she teased. "It would be so much more fun with you."

"Mm. I'm sure you'd like to watch me die, babe." I steered her into the interrogation room ahead of me, slammed the door shut behind us, and checked yet again that the recording was off. We were completely alone here.

I shoved her deeper into the room to put some distance between us—because god, even when she was snarling at me, being close to her left me hard—and leaned against the door I'd just closed.

"I don't intend to watch you die at the front, though." I flashed her a smile. "Seems a bit too easy, doesn't it?"

She watched me warily from the center of the room, her hands hanging loose at her sides as if she were ready for a fight. "Nothing about being a Nephilim is easy."

"God, you're all so angsty. Don't you ever get tired of whining? We all live in a ruined world." I raked my hand through my hair as I stalked toward her.

She met my gaze, fire blazing in her eyes, and the laugh that escaped her was so acidic it burned my ears. "Oh, poor, poor, privileged angel," she said. "It must be hard having every advantage in the world laid on a velvet cushion at your feet. I'm sure that fucking compares to living in Halftown."

"I lived there, too," I reminded her.

"By choice," she shot back, crossing her arms and glaring.

I couldn't deny that. My life hadn't been the one she described, but I'd never face the particular hardships she and the twins had. They had all the problems I did, plus the hardship of being born into this world as expendable Nephilim. I'd never experience what they had. I wasn't one of them, and I never would be.

I shook my head and stared back at her, changing the subject rather than acknowledging my privilege. "You could beg for my help, you know. To keep you from the front."

"You want me to think you're the big bad wolf who can offer me mercy, Noah, but you're just another one of the Warden's dogs and you'll do as he tells you." She offered me a cool smile. "Do you get treats? Belly rubs? Or just the opportunity to not be kicked around? *Good boy, you're better than those Nephilim...*"

She couldn't rile me. Hell, she was right to some extent. Angels loved believing they were better than Nephilim, just like Nephilim thought they were better than humans. That desperate arrogance made them easier to control.

"The warden's not actually my boss," I said. "I work for Michael, investigating Nephilim crimes."

Jacob, the warden, was a pain in my ass. But I had to play nice with him because I needed access to the Nephilim here. More than that, I tried to keep him happy to protect Rhyland and Beckett. If Michael ever granted me the chance to start my own team of Nephilim, like I wanted, I could save their lives. Michael was skeptical though, and so was the warden, as much as he wanted his own son to take my place as security team leader.

"Why are you telling me all this like I care about your life, Noah?" She was feigning boredom, but I knew Brianna never missed a detail. I was sure that brilliant mind of hers was whirring along.

The two of us were standing so close that I could see the rise and fall of her chest, could smell the faintest scent of her sweat after training. Even when she was freshly sweaty, Brianna never smelled bad to me. I used to love to train with her, to kiss her sweat-beaded, glowing face and shoulders after, the two of us losing ourselves in each other right there on the training mats...

I reached past her and tapped my fingernails against the cold metal tabletop. "Didn't look at what's on the table, did you?"

Her eyes dilated with just a bit of fear, but she took her sweet time looking down at the tabletop.

No Uriel's Blade. Just a stack of files.

"Unfortunately, we've only one Blade in twelve, and it's been taken out on a mission," I said. "So you and I will have to do this the old-fashioned way."

"What's *this?*"

"Before you go," I said, "I'd like to make sure all your crimes are accredited to you. So someone else doesn't pay for them."

She frowned, as if she were trying to puzzle out what trick I was playing.

"I know how little you care about leaving others to suffer for your sins," I said, and her eyes tightened with fury. "But maybe you'll want to ease your conscience before you die. And it will buy you another week or two here before you march off to your death."

I let my gaze roam her face. "After all, I have more important duties outside the prison. I don't have every day to spend going through your list of sins. So you can enjoy our hospitality here in Twelve a little longer."

While I tried frantically to get my Nephilim team. It had been a done deal a while ago—before Beckett's antics started a riot, pissing off the warden, and he started fighting my plan, pushing back when Michael seemed inclined to approve it.

It was very fucking hard to save the two of them, and sometimes I thought maybe I should give it up. All this work and then they'd probably knife me in the back. With Brianna added, that made it even more unlikely. She'd already somehow killed one angel. I was sure she'd do her level best to end me, too. Not that I could blame her.

"I don't mind confessing," she said, crossing her arms and glaring. "But I don't want to do it with you."

"There's just me, baby girl," I told her. No one else gave a damn. But what I said was true—if I didn't close all these open cases, some other Nephilim was likely to be tagged with one of the crimes. Especially if they needed a reason to drag some poor inconvenient Nephilim in here.

"Sit," I ordered. When she just stared at me, I started to reach for her, but she jerked away.

"Don't touch me, Noah," she said, moving to her chair. She took a seat, crossing her arms over her sports bra as she leaned back. That was my Bri—always looking as if she owned the place, as if were perfectly confident. Especially if she shouldn't be.

Part of me wanted to try to tell her everything. But it was so complicated. When my gaze fell to the nearly-healed wounds on her arm, which she scratched absently, I knew she'd never believe me anyway.

CHAPTER TWENTY-TWO

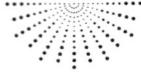

B*rianna*

"WHEN DOES the prisoner transport usually come?" I asked as we headed for the showers after a long day of training.

Beckett smiled mirthlessly. "You never know," he said. "Whenever they need more cannon fodder on the frontlines."

"Damn," I muttered. "No way to plan ahead then."

"That would be too easy," Rhyland said. "If we knew when they were coming, we might get too comfortable. The angels want us in a constant state of fear. It's easier to control us that way."

"Psychological fuckery is their specialty," Beckett said with a grimace that made the scar running down his face crinkle as if to illustrate his point.

"So, we just have to wait?" I clarified.

Rhyland nodded. "Wait and wonder if we're next."

Except this time, we knew we were next. We just didn't know when that would be.

"The way they do it, it's almost like a sting," Beckett said. "They've come running in during the middle of the night, dragged people from their beds, thrown them kicking and screaming into the transports."

"Other times, they line them up in an orderly fashion after breakfast," Rhyland said. "Like they're regular soldiers. Just depends on who's in charge that day and what power trip they get off on."

"Let me guess," I said, rolling my eyes. "Noah's the orderly one?"

Beckett's expression darkened, and his voice was laced with bitterness. "He's always been good at faking it, hasn't he? Whether he's pretending he's one of us, or pretending we're regular soldiers and not prisoners, you can't trust anything that assholes says or does."

I couldn't help but wonder, who was he pretending for?

"Think of me while you shower," Rhyland said with a wink as they stopped at the door to the women's showers. I rolled my eyes, but I couldn't help the warmth from creeping into my cheeks. I may not think of the twins in a public shower, but I'd had my fair share of fantasies in my bunk after lights out since my encounter with Beckett. Unfortunately, opportunities alone were few and far between.

Inside the showers, I spotted Anna, Erelah, and Samarah eyeing me, but I ignored them. If they had nothing better to do than gossip like petty high school bitches, I had no time for them. I was busy trying not to die. I stepped into the shower, not caring that there was only cold water left. I'd gotten plenty hot on the training grounds today. My muscles were sore and tired, and I was ready to wash away the sweat before passing out in my cell for the night.

I kept an eye on the girls, though, not turning my back until it was time to shut off the water. The moment I turned, I heard quiet footsteps in the water on the floor behind me. That bitch thought she could sneak up on me. I spun back just as Anna barreled into me, shoving me hard with both hands. She threw me back against the shower wall, but I was ready. My back hit the concrete hard enough to knock my breath out, but I kept my head forward, so I didn't hit my skull. Fuck if she'd knock me out.

I grabbed her arms before she could step back from pushing me. Using her momentum against her, I swung her around, slamming her into the shower wall. She shrieked in anger, trying to pull away. I was about to throw her to the floor when a body smacked into me from behind. Samarah leapt onto my back, grabbing a handful of my wet hair and wrenching my head back. Pain ripped across my scalp, and I stumbled backwards. Twisting sideways, I used her weight for leverage and swung my body around, slamming her against the wall. My own shoulder connected, too, but I managed to dislodge the bitch.

By now, the other girls in the room were cheering and yelling, excited by the prospect of drama to break up the monotony of life inside the prison walls. I grabbed Samarah and hurled her to the floor before she could recover her balance. Just as I turned, Erelah stepped in, throwing a punch. I ducked and brought my knee up. She folded over it, and I boxed her in the ear and dumped her on top of her friend. But just as I spun toward Anna and blocked her fist with my forearm, Samarah's foot shot out, and she slammed her heel into my kneecap.

I let out a burst of curses as pain drove into my leg like a spike, and my knee wrenched to one side. Before I could recover, Anna threw a right hook, catching me square in the jaw. I dropped to the floor, rolling away before they could hit me again. The crowd parted, letting us continue our fight as Erelah dove after me. She leapt onto me, and I bucked her off, rolling us across the wet cement floor as our fists flew.

I could have taken down any one of those bitches with one hand behind my back, and two any other day. But three was a lot, even for me. Every time I got the upper hand, one of the others dove in. I finally got Erelah down and slammed her head to the floor hard enough to make her body go limp. Before I could so much as get bearings, Samarah grabbed my hair and kicked me in the spine. A savage curse tore from my throat, and I bucked and twisted.

She hurled me off Erelah and sent me toppling across the floor. I slammed into the door to the shower room, my head spinning from the blow as the door flew open into the hall. Anna leapt at me, and the next second, she was straddling me, pinning my hands to the floor. "Get her," she yelled, and Samarah rushed over and began kicking me savagely in the ribs.

I bucked my hips, rolling sideways to dislodge Anna. Pulling back a fist, I punched her in the face so hard I felt her nose cave. She screamed with fury, falling away from me and grabbing her face. I was almost up when a sharp kick to the head sent blackness blooming across my vision. I fought for breath as Samarah's heel slammed down on my head again, stomping it against the concrete floor.

I was vaguely aware of a commotion in the hall, where we'd landed when I knocked Anna off me. Guys crowded in around us, chanting and cheering. I threw an arm up to block the next kick, but it never came. I turned just in time to see Shade shove through the crowd and grab Samarah around the throat. With a vicious twist, he spun her head around. A sickening crunch filled the air, and he dropped her body on the floor next to mine.

Without a second glance at her, he grabbed my hands and yanked me to my feet. I swayed, still trying to gain full comprehension of what had just happened. Shade reached for Anna, but she shrieked and scurried backwards on her hands. "She attacked me," she shrieked, still holding her nose. Blood poured out between her fingers.

Suddenly, a blast of cold air shot down the hall, so intense everyone stumbled back. The air blew harder, flattening everyone against the wall. Shade stumbled back, gripping me against his hard, broad chest. I was flattened against him as his back hit the wall.

A second later, Noah came striding down the hall, his hands held out to either side as he continued either making the forcefield or controlling some unseen system to keep prisoners in place when they acted up.

"What the fuck is going on?" he demanded, his eyes landing on the one person who hadn't moved. Samarah's naked body lay crumpled on the floor, looking small and insignificant out there alone. I knew what she'd been capable of, though.

Noah stopped and looked down at her for a second before raising his eyes to the rest of us. His voice was low and cold when he spoke again. "Who did this?"

His eyes moved along the row of prisoners on one side of the hall and then the other. When his gaze landed on me, his eyes widened just a fraction. I was glad for the small protection Shade's arms offered my naked flesh, but it wasn't much. Noah could clearly see I wasn't wearing anything, even with Shade's thick arms wrapped around my body.

"I did," Shade said after a long beat of silence.

"Release that prisoner," Noah ordered.

"Oopsie," Shade drawled, taking his sweet time in dropping his arms from around me and sparing a glance at Samarah's broken body. "Guess I messed with the wrong girl. Is she your slave of the week?"

Noah's eyes raked over my body, and I could see his Adam's apple bob as he swallowed hard. Without Shade's arms around me, I was on full display for everyone in the hall to see, Noah included.

"Go get dressed," Noah said, his voice indifferent despite the heat I could see in his gaze.

"He was breaking up the fight," I said quickly. "He didn't murder her."

"What fight?" Shade said, his dark eyes giving me a warning. "I didn't see a fight."

But what were they going to do to me for fighting? Send me to my death at the front? Oh, wait, I was already on my way there.

"He defended me," I said. "They attacked me."

"She's lying," Anna hissed. "She's the one who started it—unprovoked. You can ask Erelah."

"If I were you, I'd think twice before fucking with Brianna," Shade said, his eyes flashing as he spoke to my attacker. "Accidents happen so easily in here."

Anna gulped, and Noah turned to me.

"I told you to get dressed," he snapped.

I opened my mouth to protest but thought better of it. Noah wasn't going to tolerate my disobedience in front of the other prisoners, and I'd already told him what I needed to say.

I stepped back into the shower room, grabbed a set of clothes from the supply of prison uniforms against the wall, and pulled them on quickly. My head was beginning to clear after the blows I'd taken.

Fuck. Shade had just killed someone in the hall. Yeah, she probably would have killed me if he hadn't, but damn.

And half the prison had just seen me naked. Including Noah, who had looked ready to eat me up when he'd seen me. My head had been too fuzzy from the blows to process it when it happened, but now that it was clearing, a pulse of heat darted between my thighs when I pictured that look again.

So, maybe he didn't hate me so much after all.

Or maybe he was just a guy who wanted to get his dick wet like every other guy who had been in the hall getting turned on by a couple of naked girls fighting. Whatever. I didn't have time to think about Noah right now. I was more worried about Shade. He'd defended me, and now I owed him. Again. And I didn't fucking appreciate owing anyone anything. I was pretty sure I already knew a way to pay him back though. Because after that little stunt he'd pulled, I was sure he was about to be sent to the frontlines with me.

CHAPTER TWENTY-THREE

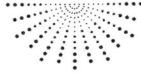

B*rianna*

WHEN I EMERGED from the shower room, my wet hair soaking my prison sweats to my back, the hall was empty except for Noah, Shade, and the body on the floor. Shade knelt against the wall, his fingers laced behind his head, a grim look on his face.

When our eyes met, he winked behind Noah's back, and a ridiculous urge to laugh rose inside me, as if we shared some secret that Noah didn't know.

"Can't stay out of trouble, can you?" Noah asked me, frowning.

"I can't get in any more trouble than I was already in," I said lightly. "I'm already headed to the front."

"Wrong as usual," he gritted out.

Two more guards appeared at the end of the hall, striding toward us. "We heard the alarm."

"It's under control," Noah told them. "We just need a cleanup crew."

He sounded bored, apathetic about the body on the floor. Completely different than he had a moment before.

"What happened?"

"You can read the report when it comes out," Noah said, sounding like as much of a jackass as I would expect, even when he talked to his fellow angels.

One of the guards stepped over the body, turned her over so he could see her face better, and then swore. He looked up, his eyes livid as they moved from me to the demon against the wall.

Leaping to his feet, the guard dove at Shade, already pulling his baton from his belt.

"It's not worth it, Jonathan," Noah warned him, grabbing his arm before he could hit Shade. "If the warden finds out you had a fuck toy among the prisoners, you'll be demoted."

The angel stared back at him. "You knew?"

"I know now," Noah said. "Get the body cleaned up. I'm taking them to solitary for fighting."

The other angel pushed Jonathan down the hall, steering him along as he looked over his shoulder as if he wanted to tear Noah apart. Noah either didn't register the death stare or didn't care.

"You know, your own angelic friends are going to slit your throat one day," I told him as he gestured to Shade to get up.

"No, they won't," he said. "Because rather than being governed by their feelings, they have some semblance of discipline and loyalty, something you would never understand." Noah sounded furious. "Now move."

I moved my feet, but that didn't mean I would stop moving my mouth. "Right, all those ridiculous human feelings we have, like love or a sense of betrayal…"

"Oh, I got to know betrayal since I got to know you, baby girl," Noah growled in my ear.

He must have forgotten Shade was there, or more likely, he didn't give a fuck about a demon overhearing. He had no idea I was anything at all to Shade. The demon didn't react in the slightest, not even a twitch to his broad shoulders, but shame knotted in my stomach. I was embarrassed at how hard I'd fallen for Noah, what a fool I'd let him make me into. I didn't want even a demon knowing I'd loved an angel.

"That's why you were eye-fucking her in the hallway," Shade said, sounding amused. "I figured she was your next victim. I know how you angels like to take out your more demonic impulses on the helpless prisoners who can't escape or fight back."

"Shut your mouth, demon," Noah growled.

Shade smirked over his shoulder. "The two of you have a past, though... Interesting."

"I'm going to keep you in solitary until you forget," Noah threatened.

"Already forgotten," Shade said, turning back around.

Noah caught my gaze and growled, "What?"

"Nothing."

"Did you do this on purpose?" Noah asked Shade, right after he'd pushed him into one of the narrow cells. "Start a fight so she'd stay here instead of going to the front?"

Shade's black eyes widened just a fraction before returning to the sardonic boredom he usually showed. "The fights always find me, pretty boy."

"Well then, consider this your vacation." Noah slammed the door shut on him.

"He didn't do anything," I told Noah.

"Why are you defending a demon?"

"I'm not," I said with a placid smile. "But you wanted me to take credit for my crimes, remember?"

Noah hesitated, like he wasn't sure if he should believe me. But Shade's expression had betrayed the fact that he had no idea I was going to the front, and at last, the angel seemed convinced. He put his hand on my lower back to propel me toward the cell. His fingers brushed across my lower spine, right above the curve of my ass, and I took a quick step forward, yanking away from his hand as if he'd burned me.

He stared at me, eyes narrowing. "You're safer in there, too.

There's a transport going to the front tomorrow, and while your name's not on the list yet, the way you piss off the warden, he might throw you on, anyway."

He waited a beat, letting that land, while my chest squeezed frantically. The guys and I needed to get on that transport—and I probably owed it to Shade to bring him, too. He'd saved my life, casual as he acted about it.

Noah looked so smug, as if he expected me to be grateful even as he fucked up all my plans. "You can say *thank you, sir*, if you want. No one will hear."

"Noah," I blurted. My mind raced, trying to think of a way to get out of this. Noah's biggest weakness was those same emotions of mine that he seemed to hate so much. I put my hands on the sides of the doorway, trying to look frightened. "You can't leave me in here. I'd rather just go to the front."

"Why would you rather go to the front?" he asked, a frown creasing between his eyes.

"You don't know what happened to me since we saw each other," I said, letting my eyes well with tears. It was truly a stage-worthy performance. I let my voice go husky—a mix of unshed tears and sex appeal, I hoped. "But I'm terrified of being trapped. Being here is bad enough, but if you force me into a windowless box, I'll lose my mind."

"Who hurt you?" he asked, fury blazing in his eyes that almost made *me* afraid.

"It doesn't matter," I said. "Just please, Noah…"

He stared at me, a tortured look written across his face. Hilarious, since he was the one who had hurt me most. Aside from maybe the angel who had murdered my mother in front of me.

Noah shook his head. His voice was brusque when he said, "Brianna, you're tough. You'll survive. But Shade killed someone today. Not just anyone, either—one of the damned prisoners that the guards have been fucking. If he's not locked down, with a camera on him, twenty-four-seven, he's going to be dead by morning."

Fuck.

"Be good," he mouthed, reaching out to wipe away one of the fake tears that rolled down my cheek. "I'll be by to check on you in the morning, and I'll be watching on the cameras if anyone tries to hurt you."

"Why do you care?"

"Fuck if I know," he said, his voice hardening in contrast to the kindness that had just filled it. "Especially when you lie to me."

God damn it. He could always read me.

He licked my tear off his thumb, gave me a shrug, and shoved me back into the cell. He was already humming before he slammed the door shut on me and sauntered down the hall.

I caught myself and stood in the midst of the tiny, bright room for a minute, trying to catch my breath. It felt like Noah had sucked all the air out of the room and pushed me off balance in more ways than the physical. When had he figured out I was lying? Had I tipped him off at the end?

I turned to take in my new surroundings. Like everything in Twelve, it was clean and bright. But the room was very small—I could reach out both arms and brush my fingertips over the white walls. There was a cot and a toilet beyond. Nothing else.

I threw myself onto the bed, propped my head on my arm, and looked up to find words written across the ceiling. *Therefore I abhor myself, and repent in dust and ashes.* A verse from Job. Nice touch—as if the angels weren't the worst sinners of all. It made me want to crack open the ceiling and turn those words into dust themselves.

"Brianna?"

I jolted upright from my trance of boredom and fury. It was Shade's low, sexy voice, right in my ear.

"Shade?" I asked, my voice a whisper in the cell. I twisted around, staring at the walls in this tiny closet around me. I was still alone. I shouldn't have heard his voice so clearly if he spoke to me through the wall. The walls would be thick down here, anyway, so prisoners couldn't communicate. We were in solitary, after all.

"Well, who knew?" He sounded amused. *"You can hear me."*

Unless I was losing my mind, just as I'd told Noah I would. I'd go a long way to win an argument, but I wasn't interested in going all the way into madness.

"How?" I whispered.

You don't need to say it out loud. Just think.

Noah would say that's not my strong suit, I thought, and Shade huffed a laugh. I felt my eyes widen. *You can really hear what I'm thinking?*

Apparently, he said. *Demons practice holding ourselves back and communicating with our minds. You're not doing a very good job of that, angel baby.*

Demons? I wasn't a fucking demon, and I was sure my horror went down the line, because I could feel him falter on the other side. Shit. I'd hurt his feelings.

I'm not that easily hurt, he said. I could hear the smirk in his voice. *I know what you all think of us.*

It's just—if we can communicate—

Then maybe fate's played quite the trick on us.

What does that mean?

I could hear his warm, sinister chuckle in my mind. *Maybe there's some other magic at play.*

Some magic that lets a demon communicate with the child of an angel?

Yes. We were quiet a moment before he spoke again. *Are you okay?*

I'm okay, I promised him. *A little banged up, but okay. Are you?*

Right as rain, he drawled. *I didn't take a single blow.*

There are other ways to get banged up besides the physical, I reminded him.

He chuckled again, that sound that was warm but so unsettling. *I don't have any feelings one way or another about killing. And she had it coming.*

Why? I asked. *Just because we were fighting?*

Because she was hurting you, he said. *You know, you don't have to get yourself injured for us to spend time together.*

His tone was sexy and teasing, and I couldn't help the flutter of excitement at the forbidden thrill of flirting with a demon. I had always been taught to fear them, but here, he couldn't touch me. It was safe, but still so taboo it made my heart pound. *I wasn't trying to spend time with you*, I protested. *And we're not even together.*

Oh, but we are.

You don't even work in the infirmary, I added. *We ran into each other there by chance.*

Wasn't that your lucky day?

His tone was still light, but I sobered at his words. Had it been my lucky day? Or his unlucky day? *Noah said you'd be in danger because of what you did.*

So I'm in danger. He yawned, and I could've sworn that through the bond, I could even feel him stretch. *Same song, same verse.*

You didn't have to do that for me.

I'm not going to let anyone hurt you, angel-baby.

Why? I'd meant to think it to myself, but the words echoed down the bond, even after I bit my lip, wishing I could take them back.

I could be pretty kickass in a fight, but I did not relish talking about anyone's feelings. And when he didn't answer, the silence stretched on until I thought it would break.

That's a damn good question, he drawled at last.

You're going to have to do better than that.

I'm... Drawn to you.

Still not sure that's gonna cut it. You went straight psycho and snapped someone's neck with your bare hands when her squad was kicking my ass. All you can give me is that you're drawn to me?

He chuckled again. *You surprise me, angel baby. It's been a while since anyone has done that. That's worth fighting for. Or at least keeping around a little longer, until I decide if it's worth fighting for.*

I smiled, and just then, the lights went out abruptly, soaking our rooms in pitch darkness. The damned words on the ceiling glowed, though, the only thing I could see.

Tell me a bedtime story, Shade, I whispered.

And even before he began to talk, I knew he would.

CHAPTER TWENTY-FOUR

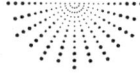

B *rianna*

IF I THOUGHT my childhood was grim, hearing about Shade growing up in literal hell made mine seem like a walk in a Paradise. I slept plagued by images from Shade's grisly tale. Apparently, he wasn't the right guy to ask for a bedtime story. Lesson learned.

I woke when the harsh, overly bright lights of the prison washed over me the next morning, still groggy but instantly alert. My heart hammered as I leapt to my feet. Noah had said there was a transport today. That meant they'd come for me when it arrived. Didn't it?

As the twins had said, there was no way to know when they'd come. The angels didn't like to tell us, maybe thinking we'd try to pull something or even revolt. There were hundreds of prisoners and only a dozen or so guards. But the angels had all the weapons, in addition to strength and powers that Nephilim didn't possess.

I sat back down on the edge of the bare bunk. If the guards took me straight to the transport, the twins wouldn't know I'd left the prison. I wasn't hopeful about my chances of surviving the frontlines, but at least they'd be safe if I was taken alone. My biggest concern was if the guards didn't take me, but the twins thought they had brought me to the transport. They'd go and get on it looking for me. Noah had acted like being in solitary might prevent me from going. If the twins got on the transport to the front, and I didn't...

Good morning, angel-baby, came a sultry voice, gruff with sleep. It startled me enough to look around, even though I knew Shade was somehow in my head and not in the room.

Do they take prisoners from solitary to the transport? I asked. *The one going to the war?*

I've been in solitary plenty, but I've yet to be sent to the front, Shade said. *I'm thinking it's a good bet we're 'safe.'*

I could hear the extra irony he put into the last word.

Damn it. How could I get a message to the twins? It would have come in real fucking handy if I could communicate with them, too.

What'd you do to get sent out so fast? Shade asked. *I've been here for years and haven't heard a single whisper about being sent to the war.*

You say that like it's a bad thing.

I'm going to die either way, he said callously. *At least out there I wouldn't die of boredom.*

You want to go die in the war because you're bored?

What's the point of wasting away in here for the rest of my life?

Is that why you did it? Here I thought you were protecting me. Maybe you were just provoking the guards by killing their toy.

Maybe so, he drawled. *What'd you do to get sent to the front?*

You think I'm going to give you tips on how to die?

Don't tell me you care, angel baby. You're too smart to do that in this place.

A little late for that, I admitted, another shot of fear going through me at the thought of the twins going on without me. *And sorry I can't give you tips on how to get sent out. They think I killed an angel a few years ago. That's why they want me dead.*

Shade didn't respond for a minute. I stared at the white wall, imagining him on the other side, staring back at me. Was he slumped on his bed with his back to the wall? Lying down with his hands crossed under his head as he stared at the ceiling?

Is that possible? he asked at last.

No. It's not supposed to be, anyway. A Nephilim wouldn't be strong enough to kill an immortal.

They're immortal, he mused. *Not invincible. Maybe they want us to think we're weak, so we'll be compliant.*

Sadly, I don't think that's the case. I've seen a bit of what they can do. Not to mention the immortal thing, and the fact that they can fly.

Yeah, Shade muttered. *Lucky bastards.*

What about you? What are you in here for?

I cut off an angel's wings.

Damn, I said, trying not to wince at the apathetic tone of his voice, like it didn't affect him at all. But then, I'd watched him snap a girl's neck with his bare hands, so I shouldn't be surprised. He was a demon, after all.

I was just the one holding the knife, Shade said. *It took a bunch of us to take the bastard down.*

What'd he do to you? I asked, realizing as I asked that I was hoping for a reason to justify this demon's psychotic act.

He was an angel.

Okay then. No reason. Just another day in the life of a demon. I was a little unsettled that I'd somehow befriended this guy, and even more so that I could communicate telepathically with him. Did that mean our minds were somehow alike enough to make that possible?

The lights flickered, and somewhere above the bowels of the prison where we were confined, I could hear doors clanking. I wondered if that was the loading dock, if the transport was pulling up. My heart flipped, and sickness churned in my belly, but I had no answers. I could only wait in this white, blind cell.

Our breakfast was delivered through the door with no opening, sliding through the solid white surface by some kind of magic. Shade and I fell to our own thoughts. I was jumpy, waiting for the moment when the guards would come for me. I waited all day, every noise making me startle. The room was too small to do more than pace back and forth a few steps until I'd made myself dizzy. The boredom was mind-numbing and endless, enough to drive anyone mad, but I couldn't relax. I couldn't even sleep the time away, since my nerves were too frayed by the thought of the twins getting on that transport without me. If they did…

I'd never see them again. They'd be gone to me forever. Who even knew which part of the war they'd be taken to. Probably the transports didn't deliver prisoners to the same place every time, and even if they did, it could be weeks before I was taken, and by then, they'd have been moved.

Or killed.

Solitary was a new kind of torture, one that admittedly I was not prepared for. By the time the lights blinked out, I was delirious with exhaustion from worrying. But the day had passed. They hadn't come for me. Noah had let it slip that they were coming, but they hadn't come for me. I collapsed onto the bed, weak with relief. Now I just had to worry about whether or not the twins had snuck into the group and been taken without me.

Need another bedtime story? Shade asked after I'd lain in bed staring at the words on the ceiling for a while. Repent, my ass.

Ha, no thanks, I said. *The last one gave me nightmares.*

Did you expect prancing ponies and daisy chains? I'm a fucking demon.

I know. I guess I just don't know much about demons. I've always been told you're the enemy. We didn't exactly study your culture beyond that.

The angels tell you that. Just like I could tell you they're the enemy. All we want is a nice place to live, even if this level is a little chilly.

And Nephilim are caught in the middle.

Humans *are caught in the middle,* he corrected. *You're toy soldiers for the angels. Or biological weapons. Whatever you want to call it.*

That's probably a fair description, I admitted. *I was literally made to eradicate your kind.*

There was a long silence, and I shifted on the narrow, uncomfortable bed. The room was too dark, with nothing but the holy words inscribed on the ceiling to see by. I imagined Beckett or Rhyland being here. How many times had they been sent to this particular psychological torture chamber with nothing to hold onto but their own thoughts?

Suddenly, I felt overwhelmed with gratitude for Shade, for him reaching out to me and letting me know I could survive this. I felt oddly close to him even with the thick wall between us.

You can tell me a bedtime story if you want, I said, turning on my side and smiling at the dark wall.

I thought my stories weren't happy enough for you. Ask your angel boyfriend if you want someone to blow sunshine up your ass.

He's not my boyfriend, I snapped. *And that's not what I'm asking for.*

Shade was silent, and I realized I'd answered too defensively for my own good.

What are you asking for? he asked after a minute.

I hesitated. I wasn't exactly the kind of person to talk about my feelings. But it was different with Shade, since I didn't have to voice my thoughts.

Thank you, I felt, as much as I thought. *For getting that girl off me. You probably saved my life. I don't know if I even thanked you.*

You can thank me when we get out of here, he said, his voice dropping to a sexy pitch.

A little thrill went through me at his words, and I pressed my knees together at the thought of doing something so forbidden. A child of an angel was taught from birth to hate and fear demons. I was born to be a weapon with one purpose—to kill demons. I wasn't supposed to talk to them, to understand them, to flirt with them. I definitely wasn't supposed to think about what it would be like to fuck one. That was like Eve spreading her legs for the snake.

Did I scare you speechless? Shade asked with a chuckle.

I was just deciding if I should be offended that you implied I'm a whore, I lied.

Not a whore. I'm not paying for it, angel-baby. You want it, too. And I'm glad you're not easily scared.

Why's that? I asked, my heart beating hard against my ribs.

He chuckled before speaking, his voice that sexy, deep drawl. *You'll understand when you see my cock.*

CHAPTER TWENTY-FIVE

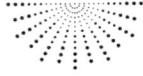

B *rianna*

THE NEXT MORNING, it seemed like I lay awake forever in the dark, staring at those damned glowing words. When the lights flipped on abruptly, I threw my arm over my eyes, but it still felt as if the walls were pressing in on me. I laid in bed for a long, long time, my stomach growling, convinced that they were screwing with us by skipping breakfast.

Then abruptly, breakfast was dropped through the door again. I sat on the edge of my bed, despite a sense of restlessness so intense it was an ache in my bones, and kicked my legs absently as I forced myself to eat the tasteless bar they'd given us for food. Or tried to. I crumpled more of it into crumbs than I actually managed to swallow. It tasted like ash in my mouth.

You doing okay over there, angel baby? Shade asked.

I didn't want to answer that. *How long do you think they'll leave us in here for?*

No telling.

I'm losing my mind, Shade, I admitted. I pictured that scene with Noah where I'd claimed I'd go nuts if I was locked up in here, remembering the flair of protectiveness in his eyes before his face shuttered and went cold, and then I felt a jolt as I realized maybe Shade could see what I'd seen. He knew now that I'd had a relationship with Noah, but that didn't stop the sense of shame from flooding my chest.

It was as if now that Shade had somehow opened the bond between us, I couldn't stop myself from pouring my thoughts down it. It was driving me nuts. I hated being that vulnerable. I didn't even tell my best friend all my secrets. And I definitely didn't tell men who were interested in being more than friends.

What difference would it make if you fucked a demon? Shade asked, laying back. *You fucked an angel, and look how that worked out.*

So that was a yes on him being able to see what I saw.

Yeah, I said sarcastically. *I'm on death row. Worked out real fucking well.*

A demon can't fuck you worse than you're already fucked, he said lightly.

Keep this line of conversation up and believe me, it won't be a temptation.

He laughed out loud. *It's a temptation?*

Well, I did just say I'm losing my mind, I admitted.

It's okay, he said. *You can admit you want me. I may be a monster, but I'm a sexy one.*

I pictured his dark eyes, that mischievous smile, his tall, powerful body, and my body thrummed with desire. I tried to push the thought away, only to feel him laugh at me down the line. At least the ache between my thighs distracted me from the misery of being trapped in this room, and then I realized...

You were pissing me off so I wouldn't freak out, weren't you?

Maybe. Maybe I like riling you up, too.

Can I just say, it's really pissing me off that you can see everything I think about, and I don't know anything you don't choose to tell me.

You can be pissed all you want, but it's a good thing I'm the only demon in Twelve... You broadcast like it's your job.

Well, there was an unsettling thought. *How do I stop?*

Now, why would I tell you that? he drawled. *This is so entertaining.*

How do you know I'd stop you from seeing if I knew how? A devilish thought of my own came to me, and I closed my eyes, remembering the view in the mirror after a shower at home. My long dark hair soaking wet around my shoulders, my face staring into the mirror; my athletic, narrow body and small, high breasts.

In my imagination, I ran my hands up my sides until I reached my breasts, massaging myself in the mirror, my nipples peeking between my fingers.

I felt Shade shudder with desire. *Keep going,* he said, his voice a raspy whisper that made goosebumps rise on my skin and my nipples pebble in more than my imagination.

The girl in the mirror smiled a small, wicked smile, and one hand slipped lower, disappearing between my thighs.

You're a bad influence, I said, breaking off the memory. *Come on, Shade. Teach me.*

Let me feel you come, he said, his thoughts rough with desire. *Then I'll teach you.*

I shifted on the bed, slipping a hand under my sweats. I stared up at the ceiling, remembering Noah saying he'd be watching. Was he watching me now? The thought of him watching me touch myself made wetness spring to life under my fingers. I bit my lips, dropping my eyes closed and moving back into the fantasy I was sharing with Shade. Was he stroking himself, too? What would Noah think if he saw us both masturbating at the same time, on opposite sides of the wall? Some spiteful part of me hoped he'd somehow guess we were thinking about each other.

I slid a finger into my tight opening, a soft moan escaping my lips. Shade groaned, and for a second, he gave me a glimpse of what his hand was feeling, his scalding skin stretched tight over a thick, ridged shaft. A shiver of excitement went through me, and I let him feel how wet I was, picturing myself in the mirror, showing him as I stroked my clit. When I pictured his powerful body entering the bathroom behind me, bending me over the sink, and penetrating me, we both started breathing hard, panting for release. He pushed into my fantasy, his own images flashing with mine until I couldn't tell which of us was creating the picture of him thrusting into me, fucking me hard until we both came. A quick wave of heat washed over me, like my skin had just ignited in a flash of flame.

I cried out in shock, my eyes flying open, my body practically sparking with electricity. I couldn't seem to catch my breath. Little sparks seemed to dance beneath my skin.

Well, Shade drawled after a few minutes. *That was fun.*

What just happened? I breathed.

He chuckled. *I think that's what you call a mind-fuck. Can't say I've never imagined fucking an angel spawn, but this was so... Interactive.*

Not that. I felt like I was on fire for a second. Was that your... Hellfire, or whatever it's called?

I don't know, Shade admitted. *Maybe.*

Did you feel it?

Oh, I felt it, angel-baby. Maybe it's the price of our sin.

Our sin?

Don't think demons are supposed to fuck angels, or their offspring.

That probably goes both ways, I admitted, feeling strangely shameful as I withdrew my hand from my pants. Picturing Noah watching had made me hot, but now, I hoped he thought it was a total coincidence. The taboo of fucking a demon was a bit beyond what I wanted him to think me capable of.

So, you gonna teach me how to block you or what? I asked.

Seeming to sense my withdrawal, Shade didn't tease anymore. Instead, he began to teach me how to put up a shield between my mind and any other demons I might encounter, in case they could read me as easily as he could. The effort kept me busy, and my anxiety at being trapped faded away. Hell, at least here I was safe to practice.

In the wastelands, once we escaped, who knew what we would run into?

As soon as I thought about that, I felt a jolt, worrying that Shade would know. Or maybe... He could come with us. I couldn't just leave him behind after what he did for us. Not to mention I didn't really want to. I hadn't admitted it to him, but I was drawn to him as well. I wasn't sure if it was just the thrill of the forbidden, or the trauma bonding, or something else entirely. I just knew I wasn't ready to let him go yet.

Getting Rhyland and Beckett on board was going to be tough, though.

Can we go back to the mirror girl? Shade asked. *She was fun.*

You don't mind my blatant attempts to make you do my bidding? My thoughts were light and teasing.

There was a silence between us for a second before Shade answered. *No one should get to walk through your mind without you choosing to allow them in. But I won't complain if you let me wander through.*

I might do that on occasion, I said, giddy with the thought of our naughty encounter earlier.

I could feel his wicked grin. *Especially when you have a little forbidden fantasy to fulfill...*

If you're a demon, how come you're good?

His thoughts sent a warning. *I'm not good. Don't make that mistake, Brianna. Don't think just because we bonded, I'm anything but a demon.*

Okay then.

His words left me unsettled. Did I think there was something special about Shade? I thought about the memories he'd shared, things that would twist anyone's mind as they grew up, and the way he shared them with his usual light-hearted amusement, as if they'd had no effect on him. But they must have. After all, he could snap a neck or saw off an angel's wings without a damn thing about it.

And yet, when I replayed the meticulous way he'd sewn up my wounds when I came stumbling into the clinic reeling with fury and stunned with pain; the way he killed my attacker to protect me; the way he'd kept me sane in solitary...

Maybe he was filled with a demon's darkness, but that darkness didn't seem to touch *me*.

But would that keep him from killing Rhyland or Beckett if he felt he had a good reason—or any reason at all? Would he kill them if he were jealous? If they hurt me unintentionally?

My mind spun, suddenly glad I hadn't revealed our plan yet. I wasn't sure what the right thing was anymore. I couldn't leave Shade behind, but what if he hurt Beckett or Rhyland?

What if Beck and Rhy were already gone, if they'd gotten on that transport?

Quit blocking me out, Shade growled, an edge of frustration in his thoughts. *I can still feel you spiraling. What's going on?*

You just told me that you're evil. What do you think?

You knew I was a demon. Did I rock your world that much by not killing you on sight? Those men of yours really set the bar low, huh?

Yeah, maybe.

How are you keeping me out?

You showed me how.

Right, but it takes years for us to learn to put up walls that thick. You seem to have mastered it in a morning.

I don't know. Maybe it's different because I'm not a demon.

I broke off as the door opened, interrupting our conversation. I scrambled up from my bed, expecting Noah on the other side.

Instead, it was Jonathan, the angel who'd wanted to kill Shade for killing his prison princess. He smiled at me, the coldest smile I'd ever seen.

"Shade," I thought. *"Jonathan's here."*

"Good news," Jonathan said. "Solitary time is over. It's back to gen pop for you."

Despite myself, as I walked out of the room and into the hall, I looked for Noah. I knew that Jonathan had some evil planned for Shade, or maybe for both of us. The kind of evil where we both ended up dead.

There was another angel out in the hall. Jonathan grabbed my shoulder and slammed me into the wall, and I let out a grunt as my forehead and nose slammed against the concrete.

"Hands behind your back," he barked, as if I'd resisted.

My impulse was to try to fight him off, but I knew I couldn't win.

All I could do was wait for my chance to escape. I put my hands behind my back, and he cuffed me roughly.

Spinning me around, he shoved me to the wall again. He nodded to the other angel, who opened Shade's door.

A moment later, Shade sauntered out, a give-no-shits look on his face, as usual. He turned, his hands held behind his back. Having seen Shade move when he decided to be dangerous, I was sure he could put up quite a fight even with those cuffs on.

Noah had said we were safe here with the cameras on us. But there weren't cameras everywhere. Not in the showers themselves. Not in the interrogation rooms. Were they taking us somewhere without cameras?

Noah claimed he'd be watching, but where was he now? Maybe he'd never meant it at all.

I knew better than to trust a single word out of his lying mouth. Apparently integrity was a virtue lacking in even angels.

"You took something from me," Jonathan murmured into my ear as he stepped intimately close behind me. "Something I liked. And you're going to replace her."

I shuddered away from him, but there was no escape.

"Not now," the other angel said impatiently. "The warden said to return them to GP."

"Not now," Jonathan agreed easily. He glanced past me, and I had the feeling he was looking at one of the cameras. I followed his gaze, my heart galloping. I was ready to try to kill him if I had to, even with the cuffs.

Brianna? Shade's voice was a whisper in my mind. *What did he say to you?*

The last thing I needed now was for Shade to go full psycho. I shook my head, refusing to tell him, and his black eyes flared with protectiveness.

I kept expecting the guards to take us somewhere else, but instead, the two angels brought us back down familiar halls to our cells. When I got back to the cell block, Rhyland and Beckett surrounded me.

Guess I'll just fuck off then, Shade murmured in the back of my mind, and then he was gone.

I sighed in exasperation. Beckett and Rhyland were not exactly compatible with Shade.

Beckett grabbed me in a crushing embrace. "I was worried about you."

"You were?" I melted into that hard chest. My heart had been pounding so hard, ready for a fight, and now I felt myself relax. The threat was over... For now.

Beckett gave me his most innocent face. "It's not like I'm a psychopath, Brianna."

I laughed at that. Rhyland was waiting beyond him, but not with any gentle, comforting hug. No, Rhyland pressed me against the bars, his hands sweeping over my body, hot and passionate, as his lips claimed mine. I clung to his powerful shoulders as his knee slid between my thighs, parting them at the same time as his tongue parted my lips, his body demanding, taking all my attention, all my thought, until every fear dropped away.

"Is there some kind of rhyme and reason to solitary?" I asked, pulling away before I completely lost my senses. "I thought we'd be there longer..."

"They like to use it to keep us off-balance," Rhyland said. "It's just like the transports. You never know how long."

"But," Beckett added, spinning me to face him. Rhyland's hands slid up my hips possessively, keeping Beckett from walking off with me. "They might've needed more space in solitary."

There was a mischievous edge in his voice, and I demanded, "What did you do?"

"Some prison princesses were smuggling in contraband, and their reign just came to an end when one of the honest guards happened to find their stash." Beckett managed to *tsk-tsk* as he shook his head, as if the whole affair were shameful. I hadn't known Beckett could *tsk.* "They'll be in solitary for a while, most likely. The warden's pretty horrified by the whole affair."

"I love you guys," I said, grinning. They were trouble incarnate.

Something flashed over Beckett's face, just for a second, before his saucy grin matched mine. "Can't let anyone hurt our girl and not pay for it."

He pulled me toward him, and my lips met his, my arms twining around his neck.

"Of course, that doesn't mean you can't pay us back," Rhyland suggested, pressing against me from behind.

I shook my head at him as their two warm, powerful bodies locked around mine, but at least their kisses and their touch let me forget what waited for us beyond these next few moments.

CHAPTER TWENTY-SIX

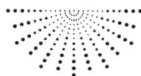

S *hade*

As I PUT in the last stitch in my busted up face, my tongue worried a tooth the guards had knocked loose in our little pow-wow the night before. I hadn't expected anything less. In fact, as I dragged my mangled carcass back toward my cell to get dressed for the day—being half beaten to death was no excuse to miss a day of work—I figured I'd gotten pretty damn lucky. No severely broken bones, at least. Probably just a few cracked ribs, definitely some bruised ones. Their boots might be fit for the angels, but they weren't made of clouds, that was for damn sure.

Or maybe they'd intentionally kept me in one piece so I couldn't miss work. Bastards. I wouldn't mind a vacation.

Solitary was the closest we came to that. It was usually a mind-fuck to be stuck in there for days at a time. Imagine my surprise when the last time, I'd thought of Brianna, and *voila!* Like magic, she answered. Shocked the fuck out of me... But in the best way.

I was thinking of her as I ambled back toward my cell, not showing how much every fucking step hurt. Being the only demon in 12 was bad enough. Showing weakness would be a death sentence. The Nephilim in here didn't know what to make of me, so they mostly kept their distance, which was fine by me. Let them think I was a psycho. I had no reason to deceive them into thinking differently.

Except for one.

As I rounded the end of the hall, I saw a commotion up ahead. A group of prisoners gathered near the loading dock. So they'd come for another round of deportations.

Damn it. I remembered something I'd plucked from Brianna's broadcast—she was supposed to be sent out on the next caravan. I shouldn't give a shit about a random Nephilim, even a hot one like her. But something about her had drawn me in from the start, though I wasn't sure what it was. Sure, there was her tough act when she'd come in after the asshole angel had sliced her up with the blade and I'd sewn her up. Or her badass fighting skills she showed in practices and even when fighting the other bitches who fucked with her.

But it was more than that. I didn't know what it was yet. All I knew was that I could communicate with her, which should be impossible. I wanted to find out more, but if they took her to the front, I'd never get the chance.

I sauntered over but stayed back from the crowd to study them. I reached out some mental feelers, seeing if I could find Brianna in the crowd. And sure enough, she didn't have her defenses up, and I could hear the woman like she had an antennae on top of her head broadcasting her every thought. Her mind was full of determination, anxiety, excitement, and nervousness.

Well, fuck me. I'd have to wade into the crowd and drag her out somehow, all without the guards seeing us. Pretty fucking impossible, but I had to try. I wasn't going to let them toss her in front of a cannon and wash their hands of her. I had too many questions that still needed answers, not to mention we'd never made that mirror scene a reality.

"We can't leave yet," she was saying to a companion. "I just need to find him…"

The dude she was with might not know who she was talking about, but I did. Her brain might as well have been screaming my name. I edged into the crowd, making my way toward her. This was going to be fun.

I jostled my way through the crowd of Nephilim, whose expressions ranged from shell-shocked to resigned to anguished. A few of them were crying. Usually prisoners in here knew not to show emotion because emotion was weakness, but I guess once they knew they were dead men walking, those rules ceased to have meaning.

Just as I reached Brianna, one of her loverboys stepped into my path. The other one, the one with a scar marring his face, clung to her side like a barnacle. If I'd stitched him up, you'd barely be able to see that cut. Instead, he'd gotten one of the actual doctors, who didn't give a fuck about anyone's comfort level, let alone scars. His brother was unmarked as the day he'd arrived, though. I wondered whose dick he was sucking to keep that pretty face.

"What are you doing here?" growled the fresh-faced one.

"Why don't you ask her, Pretty Boy," I said with a smirk, my gaze cutting to Brianna.

"What is he doing here?" Scarface asked Brianna, his eyes fixed on me and his voice low and cold.

"He's coming with us," Brianna said, lifting her chin to the two Nephilim.

"Like hell you are," Pretty Boy said to me, still blocking me from Brianna.

"Shade is a good ally," she said.

I cocked a brow at her and smirked. "If that's what you want to call it."

Scarface stepped forward, but Brianna grabbed his arm before he could do anything stupid, like start something he couldn't finish. He was just a little Nephilim. I was a fucking demon. I could eat him for breakfast. I wasn't scared of his punk ass. "He defended me when

Anna was about to kill me," Brianna said, her voice low. "If this is how I repay the favor, then I owe him this much."

"Fine," Pretty Boy said. "We get him out the gates, and that's it. We cut ties there."

My gaze met Brianna's, and I could feel her conflicted emotions. She wanted me with her, but she didn't want us fighting, and she didn't think we'd ever accept each other. I wasn't making any promises. If anyone fucked with me, they got what they had coming. Simple as that. I wasn't going to bend over for anybody, not even her loverboys. I'd just met the girl, and yeah, she was hot, and she intrigued the fuck out of me. But I wasn't ready to sell my soul, little as a demon soul with worth.

"What happened to you?" she asked, stepping past Scarface to touch my cheek.

I shrugged. "Guards were a little grumpy last night. It's just a scratch."

She scoffed. "A scratch? Your eye is swollen shut, and it looks like your nose is broken."

"Which makes him a liability," Scarface said. "As if a demon won't be noticeable already."

"What's it to you?" I asked. "If I get on this transport, I get killed on the frontlines, just like you."

"You're fucking with our girl, that's what," Pretty Boy said, puffing up like that was going to intimidate me.

I cocked a brow at him. "If you check with Brianna, I think you'll find she's her own girl. And if I know her at all, you're not going to change her mind, so let's be done with the posturing and figure out how to get on this thing without being on the list."

The two cocksuckers looked like they wanted to strangle me, but Brianna held up a hand. "He's right," she said. "We can worry about everything else later."

Like whether they were going to ditch me.

"What the fuck, Bri," Pretty Boy muttered.

Brianna was broadcasting their escape plan loud and clear. Good thing there were no other demons around. So, maybe I'd just tag along on their escape from the convoy. Once we were on board, it would be easy enough to follow them off. I was determined to find out why I could hear Brianna's thoughts, why she could hear mine, and why I felt that unsettling connection to her.

We shuffled forward with the rest of the prisoners headed down the chute that pretty much amounted to death row. When we reached the bottom of the ramp, there was an angel with an uptight expression holding some kind of gleaming golden tablet with names carved onto it. I knew one swipe of her hand would erase this truckload of names once we were gone, wiping our blood from her hands as if we'd never existed.

"Name," the woman said, sounding bored.

"Brianna Chermaine," the raven-haired Nephilim said, handing over her orders to the guard.

"Brianna Chermaine," the angel said, making a mark on her tablet. "Go ahead."

Pretty Boy stepped forward as if to follow, but the angel held up a hand. "Name?"

Scarface edged to her side, trying to steal a glance at her tablet while Pretty Boy spun some ridiculous story.

"We were caught at breakfast," Pretty Boy went on. "Maybe you don't have us on there? I guess it was all misunderstanding. I'll just head on back, then."

"Oh, you're getting on. Name?" repeated the angel, looking annoyed. Brianna hovered behind her, as if torn whether to board without her boy toys. Scarface edged closer, trying to get a better look at the tablet. The angel shielded it with a hand, turning to glare at him.

"Need a reason to send us to the gallows?" I growled.

It seemed like a good time for a distraction, so I turned and smashed my skull into the face of the nearest Nephilim.

Go! I shouted to Brianna in my mind as the angel tucked her tablet under her arm and yanked her baton. The guard and a bunch of prisoners went nuts, but I lifted my head long enough to see Brianna grab her men and get going before the mob dragged me under. By the time they dragged me from the fray, I was glad to see no sign of Brianna or her little fan club. I could only hear her echo of "Thank you," in my head.

"You," the guard barked, pointing at me while a half dozen Nephilim held me. "What's your name?"

I gave her a grin and a fake salute. "It's Shade, ma'am."

"You just signed your own death warrant," she snapped, stomping over to snap a pair of icy cuffs on me. They seared into my skin like a brand, and I gritted my teeth against the pain.

"Is that really necessary?" I drawled. "You're already sentencing me to death."

"A demon doesn't deserve to even ride to his death in comfort," she snarled. "On the truck, hell boy."

I gave her a vicious grin and headed for the truck, right where I wanted to be.

CHAPTER TWENTY-SEVEN

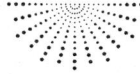

B*rianna*

BECKETT SLID into the seat beside me on the transport, which left Rhyland giving him a sour face as he took the seat behind. Typical. We were making a play that might very well get us all killed, but boys could still take time to be jealous.

The transport was filling rapidly and some prisoners standing in the aisle glanced at the empty seat, then away, but everyone gave Rhyland a wide berth. If I hadn't been so nervous, I would've teased him. The man looked like a psycho, but he was a marshmallow on the inside.

Then Shade threw himself into the seat next to Rhyland. Of course the only guy more psychotic than the twins was the only one who wasn't scared to sit with them. He shot me a cocky grin. "You cause me nothing but trouble, angel baby."

Rhyland twisted in his seat and stared at Shade in dismay. I think the man was actually shocked speechless for the first time in his life.

"What the fuck do you think you're doing?" he finally managed, an edge in his voice.

"Saving your genius plan from the fiery obliteration it deserved," Shade drawled. "You're welcome."

Rhyland narrowed his eyes. "I'm sure smashing someone's head apart was a real sacrifice for you."

"Actually, I enjoyed it," Shade said with a grin, adjusting his position so he was lounging comfortably in the seat. "Killing can be a rush if you're in the right frame of mind."

"Don't tempt me," Rhyland growled.

"Shut up, Rhyland," I whispered, making sure no one else could hear. I didn't want to ruin his fearsome reputation by having everyone listen to me tongue-lash him, but I wasn't putting up with his shit, either. Not now.

Rhyland's eyes widened for a second, then narrowed in anger, and he leaned forward.

Shade tensed ever-so-subtly, like he was ready to spring, and I had a feeling he'd be more than happy to snap his neck if he talked to me in a way the demon didn't like.

Sweet thought, but I didn't need saving.

I went on before Rhyland could interject, "Shade just sacrificed his life for us. He wasn't supposed to be on the death transport in handcuffs, was he?"

"Thanks for the support," Shade said, flashing that scary grin at me. "Need me to get rid of these two assholes, too?"

"They're good," I said with a smirk. "But I'll let you know."

"Sure thing, angel baby."

"Can you stop calling her that?" Rhyland snapped, turning to Shade in irritation. But the tension between them that had felt like it might flare into bloodshed was gone.

This was just Rhyland's natural and unavoidable level of dickheadedness.

"You'll get used to him," I promised Shade.

Rhyland scoffed, and Shade shrugged, looking unaffected. I raised my eyebrows meaningfully at Beckett, who grinned back at me as if he knew what I was thinking. Rhyland probably had more in common with the demon than he wanted to admit.

"I can't wait to see your brilliant plan play out," Shade said. We couldn't exactly tell him what the plan was now that we were here on the transport.

But then, maybe I didn't need to tell Shade anything. He could read my mind, after all.

"You'd better hope it does," Rhyland said. "You're not going to last long otherwise. They're not going to send a demon into battle."

I hadn't even thought about the fact that now that Shade was here, they'd probably just kill him rather than send him into battle. Neither Nephilim nor angels would want a demon watching their backs.

"Their loss." Shade yawned and settled back into his seat as if unfazed by the thought of is own death. "I wouldn't mind unleashing on either side."

"Wait." I stared at him, thinking about his story of sawing off an angel's wings. "You don't like the demons, either?"

He shrugged. "There are no heroes in this story..." He glanced at Rhyland out of the corner of his eye before adding, "...angel baby."

Rhyland rolled his eyes and turned his head to look out the window.

Shade had told me a few snapshots from his childhood in a light-hearted tone, and he seemed to take those horrible moments in stride. But they must have affected him more than he let on.

I didn't realize I was accidentally picturing a young, innocent Shade in my mind, who was brutalized and alone in Hell, until he gave me a look. I'd felt an instant pull to protect him, but of course the past was long over.

Just like I was *long over* that moment when the angel snapped my mother's neck in front of me, right?

Shade leaned forward. *We're different people now, Brianna. Neither of us is a victim.*

His voice was low and certain—and all in my head. Beckett looked at him as if he wondered what the hell was going on between us. I wasn't about to explain my telepathic connection with the demon, especially on the transport where others could overhear. I was pretty sure it was not normal, and I didn't want to be singled out any more than we already had been. The last thing we needed was to draw attention. We'd let a demon sit with us and talk to us. That was already risky enough.

Even when we're here, Shade said in my mind. *The odds look terrible, but this whole fucking world is our choose-your-own adventure, and we decide who we are and when we die.*

I wished I was certain of our power in this situation. When I looked into Shade's magnetic black eyes, a sense of strength and peace washed through me, one that I was pretty sure had nothing to do with trauma bonding or our sexy solitary adventures.

He winked at me and flashed that deranged smile, which had Beckett frowning as he glanced between us, obviously trying to figure out what was going on.

God, I had to get better at putting up my walls. I imagined them slamming into place around me, and Shade sighed and slouched back in his seat.

Beckett elbowed me and muttered, "Could you stop eye-fucking the demon for like, two minutes?"

I rolled my eyes. I wasn't going to argue with him because I didn't want to explain what I was really going to do. It would have to wait until we'd escaped. Then we could explain... If we all made it out alive.

"Don't worry, Beck, you'll always be my number one," I crooned, laying my head on his chest. His big arm circled my shoulders, cuddling me close.

I knew which of the foul-tempered psychopaths behind me kicked my seat in retaliation, but it just made me smile. Rhyland was still such a kid in some ways.

"Damn right," Beck murmured into my ear.

We spent all day in the transport. There was a single bathroom stall in the back of the bus, watched over by a guard. I almost smiled wondering who he had pissed off. It had to suck to be an angel blessed by the almighty and spend your day guarding a toilet. They didn't bother to feed us, which made the rumblings of discontent even worse. But the angels didn't have to eat like we did, so they didn't always think about little things like keeping us alive.

As the sun was setting, we left the cities behind and began to roll through the vast wasteland that separated the occupied parts of the city from the front. Burnt-out, ruined human cities dotted the landscape. The first demon attacks had come fast, too fast to save this territory or any of the humans in it.

A gorgeous sunset flamed across the sky. Then night settled in, heavy and dark, pressing down on us. The transport went dark. I started to doze with my head against Beck's shoulder. Unpleasant dreams crowded me, dreams about the academy, what happened before that with my mother, and about the good days, too. Somehow those were almost worse, remembering that she loved me. Those memories always led me back to the terror in her eyes when the angels found us.

A sudden lurch to a stop woke me. I jerked upright, yanked out of my dreams. Floodlights came on from the front of the transport, bright and blinding, and everyone threw up their arms to block the light from their eyes.

"Let's move," the guards barked. "If you want a meal and a bed for the night, you need to be off this transport in the next two minutes. Stragglers sleep in the yard."

So we'd finally made it to the refueling center. I was bounced between bodies as I made my way through the transport, glancing back through the crowd. I'd been pulled away from the guys, and I had to find a way to get back to them. We had to stay together now. This was it—our chance to escape.

I stepped down from the transport into a little slice of hell on earth.

The remnants of a city spread out to either side of us. High walls surrounded us, keeping us from the questionable freedom of the dead zone beyond, along with ugly rows of metal shipping containers and concrete barriers. Ash and shards of metal crunched underfoot, reminding me that I was walking on the dust of buildings, homes, even humans. There had once been a thriving society here. Now the air carried a heavy acrid scent, as if what had happened here had tainted the land forever.

Even the angels hadn't managed to put a fancy spin on this place. Sometimes I wondered how much they'd cared about the *saving* part of the human situation.

Now, in the chaos, Shade whispered into my mind. The angels were herding everyone toward a set of shipping containers that would doubtless be our home for the night. The first few people in the front of the line were already catching individually packaged bags of foods that two guards threw at them as they entered the units. My stomach growled, and I thought how great it would be to have one of those packages of food and water before braving the dead zone. But Shade was right. If we were locked in those shipping containers, we'd lose our chance.

The guards were counting prisoners as they went in, making sure the numbers matched their manifest list.

Hey, angel baby, Shade's voice whispered in my mind. *What do you say we ditch those assholes and make a run for it?*

You mean my friends, who risked their lives to be on this transport with me? I clarified. *I think they'd make a case for doing the same to you.*

The more of us run, the more likely we are to get caught.

If we're smart, we can all make it out.

There was a disturbance in the crowd to my right, people trying to duck out of the way of someone else and stumbling into each other. I already knew who it was before I glimpsed Rhyland slamming through the crowd like a bullet, with a determined, hostile look on his face.

I grabbed his hand in mine and clung tight. I didn't have to turn around to look for Shade; I could feel him in my mind, lurking a bit behind me and to our left, looking for the right place to hide.

There. If we use the crowd as cover and move behind that shipping container, that construction area looks abandoned, I thought, letting him hear me loud and clear. We had to move fast, while the crowd would still hide us from both the angels behind on the transport and the angels ahead at the shipping containers. But...

"Where's Beck?" I asked Rhyland.

He twisted, looking for him in the crowd. "I don't know. I've been trying to find both of you."

I've got eyes on him, Shade said. *But the minute they notice the count is off, they'll be mutilating our corpses with their heavenly blades.*

Not leaving him, I thought back, annoyed. I started to turn toward the crowd, pushing back through.

What are you doing? Shade barked.

Getting Beckett.

You mean getting yourself killed?

I'll get your fucking pretty boy, Shade growled. *Get to cover. Now!*

Rhyland was going to hate that idea. I wasn't even sure I liked it. Shade had just suggested we ditch my guys. But we were going to draw attention if we fought against the tide of prisoners.

"How much do you trust me?" I whispered to Rhyland.

Before he could answer, I dragged him hard to the left toward the shipping containers. He hesitated, then made a decision, bobbing and weaving with me quickly into hiding. Once we were behind the shipping containers, the two of us ran for the construction area, stumbling over bits of metal and debris that stuck up from the charred, melted landscape.

Then we were in a dark pit where a foundation would be poured, enormous figures of cranes and other construction equipment jutting into the smoky, black, starless sky.

Rhyland turned to face me. "All right, Brianna. I trusted you. Now where the hell is my brother?"

CHAPTER TWENTY-EIGHT

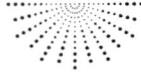

B*eckett*

I SEARCHED the crowd frantically for any sign of Brianna or my brother, but the only person I recognized was the demon who had attached himself to our girl for reasons I could guess all too well. What I didn't know was why the fuck she hadn't ripped his nuts off and told him where to stuff them. That was the Brianna I knew and loved. Not the one who went around collecting hell spawn.

The demon shoved past a girl who squeaked and scurried out of his way like he'd burned her with his touch. For all I knew, he had, being a demon and all.

Damned if it didn't look like he was coming straight at me. I tensed, holding my wrists apart in front of me, the cuffs binding them together. I could probably get them over his head and strangle the bastard if he fucked with me. He probably had the same idea, and he was taller, so he had an advantage. The thought only pissed me off more. If he knew anything about where my brother and Bri had gotten off to, so help me...

"I know what you're looking for," he growled in that creepy voice of his, like leathery wings beating.

"So does every other person here," I snapped. "Want a fucking gold medal?"

"Shhhh," he hissed. Between the voice and the inhumanly dark eyes, it was all I could do not to shiver. Like everyone in 12, I avoided the demon like the plague he was. I might have had a short fuse, but I didn't have a death wish.

Where the fuck were they? I knew they wouldn't bunk down for the night without finding me—not on purpose, anyway. But the guards were marching us toward the container cars all too fast.

"Come on, Scarface," the demon said, reaching out like he'd grab my arm.

I drew back. "What do you know?" I whispered under my breath, glancing around from the corner of my eye. The demon was already drawing enough attention without me swiveling around like I was looking for something. I didn't know the other prisoners personally, but they were all miserable shits like us. They didn't owe the angels any loyalty if they overheard us, but you never knew what someone would do for an extra food ration.

"I know if you go into that box, you're never seeing her again," the demon said. "Doesn't matter to me. I won't be there. Get in that car, no one will even notice we're gone. Works out better for us."

It took about half a second to do the math in my head. There were three extra people on the transport—the demon, my brother, and me. He should be the one getting in the shipping container. But somehow, he'd wormed his way into our escape plan, and somehow, Brianna had agreed.

"Move, move," yelled an angel guard, jogging down the side of the crowd, trying to herd us into a line to get in the makeshift bunker.

"Can't say I didn't try," the demon muttered, then turned and stalked off. I saw where he was headed, but now that the crowd had bunched together, he had to cross an open space before reaching the machinery that they must be hiding behind. Fuck.

I skirted along the edge of the crowd, only to hear a shout from up ahead. "Hey!" one of the guards barked. "You there." I glanced over my shoulder, but he wasn't looking at me. He was looking at Shade, who had made it about ten paces from the group before he caught the attention of a guard. It was hard to ignore a demon.

He must have known that. So either he was creating a distraction again so I could get away while he was killed—because why wouldn't the guard just get rid of the hassle here and now?—or he had risked his neck to find me and tell me where to go. And now he was about to pay for it with his life. The only difference between the two scenarios was that in one, he hadn't meant to sacrifice his life. I figured that was the correct theory. Demons weren't known for their selflessness.

So what miracle had made him risk his life to come get me? It had to be Bri. She wanted me to know where she'd gone, and she'd made this demon come back to tell me. Which meant I couldn't let him get his head sliced off without incurring Bri's wrath.

As the guard jogged our way, I turned, raising my cuffed hands and doing the only thing I could think off—the same thing the demon had done. I spun around, slamming my fists into the nearest pair of Nephilim, throwing in some colorful words about them pushing me in line. Not ten seconds later, a brawl had broken out. It didn't take much to agitate a bunch of pissed off, terrified prisoners who knew they had nothing to lose because they were about to die anyway. Add to that the hunger fraying everyone's nerves, and it was almost too easy.

One of the guys came at me while another stumbled back into a different cluster. They all jumped on him for hitting into them while I ducked the asshole coming at me. I grabbed the back of his head and slammed my knee into his gut, hurling him to the cracked pavement. A guard was yelling at us, already dragging fighters apart. I glanced up and saw that the demon had made a run for it, but he'd stopped at the corner of the building. He stood watching, as if waiting for me.

How the fuck had Bri managed to get a demon by the balls?

I started that way, only to feel a heavy body slam into my back. I went down, catching myself with my cuffed hands. Shards of broken glass bit into my palms before I rolled away and onto my feet. An angel came at me with a club raised, and I lifted my hands to block the blow, knowing better than to hit him. He might not kill me quite as nonchalantly as he would a demon, but they didn't need soldiers bad enough to keep a mutinous Nephilim alive.

I gritted my teeth against the pain as the club hit my hands. I felt the bones crunch, but I kept my hands up, signaling that I wasn't involved in the fight. The angel didn't seem satisfied with my display, and he slammed the club into my skull the next time. I staggered but kept my feet. He raised the club again, but instead of swinging, he froze. I saw the flash of light reflected in his eyes before the sound hit us. The boom of an explosion rocked the pavement. Some Nephilim screamed, and a few scattered instinctually or hit the ground.

I spared a second to look over my shoulder. Across an expanse of broken pavement, the container car at the end of the line had gone up in flames.

The angels started shoving and yelling, swinging their clubs at whoever was nearest, trying to drive us all into the open sleeping car. In the chaos, the guard who had been beating me forgot who he was hitting and started shoving another group forward while another went running after the few who had scattered. I used the chaos to sprint toward the corner where the demon had been. When I reached the corner, I slammed straight into him. He'd been hovering just behind the corner in the shadows, not even leaving enough room for me to step into the darkness. He stumbled back, but not before I saw the flecks of hellfire burning in the depths of his black eyes.

"You did that?" I hissed.

"Just a parlor trick," he said, turning and loping off into the darkness. "You're welcome."

I heard shouts behind us, and I didn't wait around to see if anyone was coming. The angels may have had their backs turned when I made a break, but plenty of Nephilim had seen me. There was nothing to do now but keep going.

"Down here," I heard a voice call, and the next second, we were dropping down into some kind of hole that had been carved out of the ground. My brother grabbed me so hard it knocked the breath out of me.

"What the fuck happened?" Brianna demanded. "You were gone for like ten minutes!"

"Little mishap," Shade said, sounding utterly unconcerned. "But they're probably going to notice we're gone in about two minutes, so we'd better scoot."

"What'd you blow up?" Brianna demanded as we scrambled back up out of the pit. Her face was worried. Until the night the angel died, Brianna was always worried about getting in and getting out of our heists without violence. Like the fucking angel on our shoulder.

"What does it matter?" Shade said. "I saved your angel baby lover-boy. Isn't that enough?"

"Thank you," my brother muttered as we crept through a forest of rusted machinery toward the wall. I wasn't sure what the plan was now. We'd had no real way of knowing where we'd stop or under what conditions, but it was the best and only plan we had at this point.

"Good news is, this isn't a wall meant to keep us out of a Paradise or inside a prison," Brianna said as we raced along it. "Which means it shouldn't be too hard to climb."

Fuck. I hadn't planned on mentioning my broken hand, but there was no way I could make it over a wall like this. It would be hard enough with cuffs on under ordinary circumstances.

I heard a commotion back at the containers, and I knew they'd noticed our absence. "I might have broken my hand," I admitted in a rush. "I can hold off the guards while you climb over, though."

"Fuck that, Beck," Rhyland said. "We'll just have to find a hole and squeeze through."

"Okay," I said. "But I'll go last. That way, if they catch us before we get through…"

"The demon goes last," Rhyland growled.

"We're not leaving anyone behind," Brianna said. "Now shut up and let's find a way of here."

The four of us raced along the wall, searching desperately for a way out.

CHAPTER TWENTY-NINE

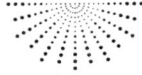

B*rianna*

"THIS IS GOING TO HURT," Shade warned.

"Why am I not surprised?" I muttered.

He held his hands on my cuffs, and the metal grew painfully hot, searing against my skin. I sucked in a breath, then the cuffs disintegrated. Shade quickly did the same for both guys. He ignored the way they stared at him distrustfully. He obviously didn't give a flying fuck what they thought about him.

This is ridiculous, Shade thought at me as we ran, putting as much distance between us and the winged pests as possible. *We're all going to die in a futile effort to save your boy.*

I leveled a look back at him. *You don't have to die. You can leave us right now.*

I meant it bitterly at first, but the more I thought about it, the more it made sense. *You don't owe us anything. You're in more danger than any of us. Just go, Shade. We'll figure something out... Or we won't, but at least you'll survive.*

Shade turned to level a disbelieving look at me over his shoulder. *You're a pain in my ass, you know that, angel-baby?*

I wasn't trying to manipulate him. He'd been treated worse than anyone back in 12. And there was zero hope for him at the front. Once we arrived, the guards would realize he couldn't be trusted and shoot him before he ever made it out of the truck—if they hadn't already done it before then.

Rhyland stopped abruptly, throwing his arms out to stop the rest of us. We all paused, the sounds of the metallic grit shifting under our feet too loud in the silent night air.

He gestured up. There was a guard tower on the wall above us, but since the guard should be focused *out* for any threats and not in, we should be safe.

"Maybe it's time we did what they think we did," Rhyland said softly.

Shade quirked an eyebrow. "Mr. Mysterious, now?"

"They think we killed an angel," Beckett said.

Rhyland nodded at the ladder tacked to the wall. The angels could fly up, but maybe they had Nephilim deliver food and messages to the guards. "I know you can get up that, Beck. It won't be fun, but..."

Beckett nodded resolutely. With his broken hand, it would be painful, but he could hook his elbow over the rungs. It wouldn't be as hard as doing a free climb.

"I'll go first," Rhy said, already heading for the ladder. "Bri, watch out for Beck."

"I'll come with you," Shade said, a sadistic smile breaking over his face. "If there are angels to be murdered, I'm in."

Rhyland gave him a skeptical look. "You know angels are almost impossible to kill."

Shade clapped him on the shoulder. "It always seems impossible until it's done."

Humming to himself, he began to climb the ladder. Rhyland

popped his eyes at Beckett and me—he couldn't believe he was working with a *demon*—before he began to climb.

Beckett and I sank into the shadows, watching for guards.

"Well, well, well," he said, his voice both dark and amused in equal measure. "You just keep adding to your fan club, don't you, Brianna? You've got your ex bag of dicks who's obsessed with you—"

"I don't want to talk about Noah."

"Too bad," Beckett growled. "I've got questions about Noah. And now you've attracted a demon. What are we going to do with you?"

"I have questions about Noah, too." I turned up my arms, revealing the now-fading scars from Uriel's blade. The moonlight reflected off my pale skin except for the darker wounds. "If he loved me, Beck, he couldn't have done this to me. Whatever was between Noah and me... It ended a long time ago."

Beckett's eyes darkened at the reminder of what Noah did to me. "If we ever have the bad luck to meet up with him again... Some day, he's going to pay for that."

"You don't need to get all violent on my behalf, Beck. I'm perfectly capable of doing violence for myself."

He smiled faintly.

"Anyway..." I elbowed him gently, mindful of his injuries. "If I've got a fan club, you're the president."

"Fuck off," he said, but he didn't deny it. He tilted his head up. Rhyland and Shade had just disappeared into the tower. We'd given them their head start. Now it was our turn. "You go first. If I lose my balance—"

"Shut up and climb," I said.

"You and I are about due for a come to Jesus meeting about your attitude *and* your bad habit of inviting extras to our party," he said, but he still went to the damned ladder. Arguing with Beckett always made me feel better, and maybe it did the same for him.

His pace slowed as we climbed higher and higher, and I caught a glimpse of his face, teeth gritted in pain. But he never stopped, and a few minutes later, we emerged into the small confines of the tower.

The angel wasn't dead, but from his bloodied appearance, he probably wished he was. Shade was on top of him, trussing him up with a rope. Angel blood was splattered all across the room, including over the windows that looked out on the barren wasteland around us. The blood shimmered golden in the dim light, and I was reminded of the pool spreading around the angel I'd thrown into the relic cases before I ran.

Rhyland kicked out one of the windows and climbed out onto the wall. He tied a rope around the window frame and kicked it out over the expanse to the ground. When it hit the ruins below, he let out a breath of relief.

"Brianna first," Beckett said. "Then you, Rhy."

Rhyland gave him a hard look. I didn't like leaving the three of them behind me, either, but we didn't have time to argue. I just had to hope they put aside their differences long enough to get out of the damned compound.

The radio started to blare. *We need eyes on the ground. We've got a prisoner missing.*

"Go!" Beckett shouted at me.

I climbed over the side of the wall, then wrapped my legs around the rope with my feet braced to act as brakes and let myself slide down as fast as I could without burning the skin off my palms. As soon as my feet touched the ground, I pulled the rope taut and stepped on the bottom, making it easier for the next one down.

Rhyland came down next, fast, then leapt free. He looked up, wild-eyed under the moonlight. Beckett and Ryland might grumble and get jealous of each other, but they also needed each other. I knew it was hard for Rhy to leave his injured brother behind with a demon.

Beckett slid down a minute later, coming down too fast because he couldn't brace himself properly. He hit the ground and stumbled back.

"I'm fine," he gritted out when Rhyland took a step his way.

I held my breath, waiting for Shade.

The shadow of a huge pair of wings fell over us, and I muttered a vicious curse. Fuck! We were caught. And Shade was still up there.

"We've got to leave him," Rhyland said urgently, grabbing my arm. "You know he'd do the same to us."

177

"Would he?" Beckett asked, looking uncertain.

What had happened up there between the two of them? Had the angel shown up before Beck started his slide down?

"Come on, let's go," Rhyland said.

Beckett picked up a rock from the ground and weighed it in his hand thoughtfully.

I could just make out two forms struggling on top of the wall, one of them winged, the other familiar in a way that made my chest ache with hope. Shade was still alive, still fighting.

Beckett whipped the rock through the air. It slammed into the angel's head, and the angel's knees buckled. Still gripping Shade, he lurched to one side. My heart caught in my chest as they teetered toward us on the wall. For a second, I thought Shade would tear himself free. But before he could untangle himself from the angel, they plummeted off the top of the wall.

CHAPTER THIRTY

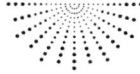

B*rianna*

SHADE and the angel hit the ground in front of us, both of them thudding to the earth with the force that would have killed a human or probably even a Nephilim. I leapt at them just as Rhyland barked my name in warning.

"Shade," I cried, yanking him free of the angel's grip, my heart racing so fast in my chest I thought it might explode. I could tell by the gruesome way their bodies were both twisted that they'd broken plenty of bones, even if both of them were still breathing. Angels had wings to avoid shit like this, but this one hadn't been able to extend his wings, either because he had been too tangled with Shade, or too injured by the rock Beckett had thrown.

Shade dragged himself free with a groan, pushing onto his knees. He leaned forward, and black blood splattered the concrete below his face. I couldn't tell if he was puking blood or bleeding from a head injury. Either way wasn't good.

Without waiting around to question him, I dove at the angel. I knew I needed a weapon, but all I had was the broken handcuffs, one metal ring still circling each wrist. Still, I knew how to fight with my fists, and there was no chance we'd get away if we simply ran from an angel, injured or not.

I leapt onto him, my knees pinning his chest. A second later, the twins had joined me. The angel writhed under us, only seeming to realize he was being attacked once we were all on him.

"Cut off his wings," Shade gritted out, his voice sounding broken and gravelly. "It robs them of most of their power."

"Only one problem with that," I pointed out. "We don't have a knife."

"I'd get you one," Shade panted. "But—" His words were cut off by a choking cough, and more blood splattered the pavement.

"Not looking so good for our demon friend," Rhyland said.

I turned back to the angel. "Your Grace," I demanded.

"Let me up," he ordered, struggling with more strength now. I knew what he was doing. He was using his own Grace to heal himself.

"I killed an angel," I warned, wrapping my hands around his throat while the twins pinned his arms. "That's why I'm here. I killed an angel with my bare hands. And I'll kill you, too."

His eyes widened, then narrowed, his nostrils flaring. "I heard about you. But it can't be true. It's impossible."

"Try me," I growled, my grip tightening.

"Before you die on us," Beckett said to Shade. "Do demons have any special tips on disposing of an angel?"

"You don't need a knife to saw off his wings," Shade rasped. "There's broken glass all around us."

"No," the guard blurted, wrenching to free himself. "What do you want?"

"Give us your Grace," I said again. "Or you die in a puddle of your own pretty golden blood."

"I need it," he whined. "I'm injured, too."

"Cry me a fucking river," Beckett snapped. "Did any of you assholes give me Grace when my face was cut in half?"

"I think we should give him the same mark," Rhyland said with a twisted smile. "It'll be our calling card."

"We're not serial killers," I snapped. "We don't need him dead. We need the Grace, and if he has to die to release it, that's what we'll do. No need to play with his carcass."

"I'll give you the Grace," the angel blurted. "Take it. It's in my hands."

I looked down to see his palms, held under the knees of the chaos twins, glowing with golden strands of light, like magic honey pouring from his skin. Lucky bastard could heal himself.

I didn't have time for jealousy, though. I needed him to heal my demon.

Reaching down, I scooped the radiant Grace from his hand, motioning for Shade to come closer. He stumbled forward on his knees before toppling to the ground beside us. I laid my hands on his skin, wincing at the cauterizing heat of it. He let out a long, low moan as the Grace sank into him.

"Heal your hand," I said to Beckett.

His lips tightened, and he gave a slight shake of his head. "The demon first," he said. "I'll take what's left."

"Not the time to be selfless, bro," Rhyland said.

Beckett answered only with a frown. I scooped the Grace from the angel's other hand before laying my palm between Shade's shoulder blades. I could feel it sinking into him, could feel his body strengthening, his muscles tightening.

"More," I said to the angel.

"That's all I have," he protested.

"Bullshit," I said, my other hand tightening on his throat. "Give us the rest, or we'll take your wings instead."

He blubbered out an excuse, but a minute later, he'd given us enough Grace to heal both Shade and Beckett. When both of them were healed, I sat back.

"Got anything to tie him with?" I asked, looking around.

I heard a sizzling sound, and the disgusting smell of burnt hair and flesh hit my nostrils just before a halfway melted cuff landed at my knee. I glanced over to see Shade gritting his teeth and wincing as he melted the other cuff from his wrist. A moment later, it landed beside us.

"Get them on him, and I'll tighten them up," he said, slowly pushing himself to his feet.

I had to turn away when the twins slipped the cuffs on the angel and he screamed as the metal burned into his skin. Shade made quick work of soldering them back together with whatever power he possessed. I didn't know much about demon magic, but I was guessing he had some kind of inner hellfire, which wasn't exactly comforting. At least it wouldn't have been if he were an enemy. Somehow, though, he'd ended up on our side.

Whatever the twins had thought of him before, they had to see how useful he was, at least. They didn't even grumble when Shade joined us a few minutes later as we stood stowed the angel under some pieces of rubble. The others would find him soon enough, but if it bought us even a few minutes, it was worth it.

"I think that's as good as we're going to get," I said. It would have been better to kill him, of course, but I wasn't sure any of us possessed that power. Yes, I'd somehow accidentally killed one once, but I still thought it must be a fluke. I'd happened to kick him into a case of relics that contained one that held something lethal to an angel, or... Something else equally coincidental.

"Then let's go," Beckett said. "No use standing around here admiring our handiwork until we're discovered."

He was right. Motioning for them to follow, I started off at an angle to the wall, knowing the angels would expect us to go straight and get as far from the enclosure as we could get. We had the whole night ahead of us, and I could only hope we'd make it far enough to find a place with a semblance of safety before exhaustion caught up to us. By the Grace of angels, my companions were healed, and all of us were strong and determined, knowing that if we were caught, this time they wouldn't send us on to the front to die.

They'd do the job on the spot.

CHAPTER THIRTY-ONE

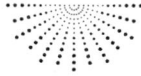

B*rianna*

WE RACED through the wreckage of the city, which alternated between abandoned buildings that still stood and craters of treacherous terrain where bombs had obliterated everything. When I turned back, I saw angels like points of light shooting into the deep blue of the night sky.

"Let's take cover," Beckett said. "We need to get into a building."

I nodded in agreement. The four of us sprinted through the eerie city streets. The place had been abandoned in a hurry, too fast even to be looted, and some of the stores were still intact. Trash blew down the streets and wild dogs howled in the distance.

Rhyland elbowed me. "You're the expert at staying invisible despite being Wanted, Bri."

I pursed my lips. "I doubt they'll go building to building for one lousy Nephilim. Not unless they think someone will hear about it and it will ruin *the good order and discipline* of their damned prison. They'll expect us to go for a house. What about going there instead?" I pointed ahead at a looming warehouse store.

"I hope there's food," Rhyland said.

"You're always thinking about your stomach," Beckett grumbled.

Shade gave me a meaningful look as the twins headed toward the building. "I'm stuck with all of you now, huh?"

"You can always go off on your own, demon," Beckett said over his shoulder without looking back.

Shade slung his arm over my shoulder, and powerful heat radiated from his body, washing over me. It felt good right now, when the evening cold was sinking into my skin. "I go where this one goes," he growled.

"I don't know how I got a demon bestie," I said, "but I guess I'll keep you."

He grinned down at me. "I'm not your friend, Brianna."

It sounded like a threat—to be fair, it was hard for demons not to sound scary—but then I realized there was something suggestive in Shade's grin. My pulse fluttered as I stared up into this strange, shimmering black eyes. He planted a kiss on my forehead and then released me, sauntering toward the building without a backwards glance.

We broke the lock and walked into the dark warehouse store, pulling the door closed behind us in case an angel passed on the street. Not that they'd notice one door open, it made us feel more protected to have the doors closed.

"God, this is creepy," I said.

Shade raised his hand, and flames rose like a torch from his palm. The flames cast light for us to see, but also threw up huge shadows around us.

"That doesn't actually make it less creepy," I said. "But thank you."

Rhyland couldn't hide being impressed. "You're like a human multi-tool," he said, shaking his head. "No wonder we're losing the war."

Beckett gave him a look, but Rhyland just shrugged. "Well, it *is* cool. I'd like to be able to make flames and explosions with a snap of my fingers. Don't pretend you wouldn't."

"Anything to make chaos," I said, rolling my eyes as I headed past an enormous pile of tires toward what looked like a hot dog stand. I jumped the counter and headed into the back. The air smelled rancid back here, and I didn't dare open any of the freezers.

"*We're* not losing the war," Beckett said behind me. "The angels are losing. We're nothing but weapons."

"Yeah, well, I don't think the demons are going to make better landlords for humanity than the angels are," Rhyland returned.

When I came back out, the guys were disappearing down the aisles. "Not like we should stay together or anything," I said, not that anyone could hear me. "We're just on the run from murderous angels who would like to kill us all where we stand. Definitely..."

Rhyland turned the corner and cycled toward me on a mountain bike.

"...do that." I finished, throwing my arms up.

But he did look pretty adorable, grinning boyishly no matter how big and dangerous he was, and I couldn't manage to be mad. He stopped the bike and leaned over to kiss me, a long, slow kiss that made heat unfurl through my body. I had to shake myself free, reminding myself of the lecture I'd started to give them. But it did feel like we'd finally caught a break.

After a few minutes, our explorations yielded plenty of shelf-stable food. We found sleeping bags in the camping aisle and set up for the night up in the shelves, hiding from the angels, just in case they made it here.

"We should've come out here to steal things," I yawned, sticking my fork into the can I was eating from. But my ravioli never reached my lips, because just then a massive blast shook the building. All of us vibrated across the shelf, the stacked boxes swaying around us.

"I hope that hit an angel," Shade said.

"More importantly, I hope it doesn't hit us," Beckett returned.

Right. That was why we never came out here to loot. It was too close to the front. The humans who had once lived here ended up squashed carelessly in the war between the demons and the angels.

It was weird to think that this store used to be full of humans, pushing shopping carts around, eating samples of chips and meatballs, and debating what kind of mattress to buy. Now they were all crammed into the city, scrounging for basic needs, while the angels ruled on high.

"Let's try to get some sleep," I said. "Maybe by morning, they'll have given up on us."

"I can't imagine anyone would be too sad about missing Shade," Beckett said, settling down on his side.

The guys' breathing settled around me. I waited for more bombs to blow, but the night had gone still after that one explosion.

"Still awake?" Rhyland asked. His raspy voice, lowered to a whisper, was sexy.

"Yeah," I admitted.

He slid closer to me. Tentatively, I lifted my head onto his chest, and he wrapped his arm around me, drawing me close. My thigh slid over his, and the feel of our bodies pressed together had heat pooling between my thighs, no matter how dangerous things were.

"Never pegged you for a cuddler," I told him.

"Never pegged you for being so mouthy," he said, then added, "Actually, that's a lie."

"Yeah, I was going to say. I think we know each other a little better than that."

The banter between us made me relax a little. I could hear his heart beating against my cheek.

"Are you really okay with Shade?" I whispered.

He huffed a sigh. "He is useful. Until he turns on us."

"So pessimistic."

"Yeah. We're both being uncharacteristic tonight," he said sarcastically.

I couldn't sleep. Eventually, I sat up. "You want to go ride the bikes around the warehouse like a pair of idiots?"

For a second, the words hung between us, and I wished I hadn't suggested something so stupid.

Then he said, "Hell yeah, I do. We're free, if only for a night. Let's make the most of it."

The two of us clambered back down the shelves, moving swiftly down them like a ladder. We went to the front of the warehouse, but the sky was quiet. We couldn't see any angels searching for us.

"Looks like it's safe-ish," I said.

"Better than we usually get."

When I turned around, he was right there. I almost ran into his hard, broad chest, and I looked up to find his handsome face staring down at me. His eyes, usually so crazy, were soft in the dim moonlight that seeped through the doors.

I raised my hand and touched his face, tracing the lines of a face I'd loved a long time ago. I wasn't sure that I'd ever really stopped. But our love was different now, not just friendship with a dash of attraction. Now there was possibility. Even though I'd been with his brother, he showed no sign of considering me off-limits.

"I'm surprised you didn't pick my brother again."

"Don't be stupid. I don't know what I'd do without your crazy—"

He interrupted me, claiming my lips with his.

I twined my arm around his neck, willing to give up name-calling for kisses. He lifted me easily into his arms and carried me deeper into the warehouse. The bikes were forgotten now. Instead, he deposited me on the edge of the first empty shelf he found. The metal bit into my ass, but I didn't care. I wrapped my thighs around his waist, holding him tight to me.

"Worried I'm going to run away, Bri?" His hand twined in my hair, pulling my head back before his lips found my throat. His kisses were demanding, claiming. "Just like that goddamn demon, I plan to stay with you."

"If you bring him up now, I'm going to think you want to bring him in on this..."

He growled, nipping my ear with his teeth, and I laughed. I leaned forward, tugging the hem of his shirt up. "We can find something else to wear in the clothing section. No more prison sweats."

"You just want to get me naked," he said, raising his arms. The dimmest light in the warehouse revealed his powerful, tattooed body, his pecs and biceps rippling with the movement.

I pushed his pants down, sinking off the shelf to slide to my knees on the linoleum in front of him. He groaned as I dragged his sweats down, his cock bobbing long and stiff in front of me. I swirled my tongue around the tip and glanced up at him mischievously to see how he reacted. He reached out and grabbed the edge of the shelf, his six-pack abs rippling above me.

I smiled before I took his cock into my mouth, delighted by the power I had over him. As I sucked and swirled and teased him, his hips rocked forward. I wrapped my hands around his thighs, yanking him toward me. My fingers dug into his muscular thighs as he groaned.

"God, Bri," he said, yanking away from me suddenly. He grabbed my waist and lifted me up, spinning me around and pushing me against the shelves. I smiled as he pressed behind me, sliding my own prison sweats down around my hips.

His cock brushed against the curve of my ass, and when his tip teased against my throbbing clit, I pushed my hips back into him. His hands tightened on my hips and he sank into me slowly, his cock filling me completely. He paused for a second, his lips devouring my neck, my shoulder. I groaned, catching his beard-stubbled jaw with one hand to turn my face to his. The two of us traded deep slow kisses with him buried deep inside me. His lips were claiming, his hands bruising. My body felt like it was on fire against his, and I was eager to let the flames consume us both.

Then the two of us began to move together. There was nothing gentle when Rhyland and I collided. He rocked into me over and over, and I bent over the shelves, slamming my ass back into him. His hands stroked over my sides, over the curve of my ass, and then he must have felt as overcome as I did because he lost himself in rocking into my body, his fingers tensing on my skin.

I heard myself moan, and I closed my eyes as pleasure rippled through my body. My core began to pulse around him, and he buried himself deep in me with a groan. "Brianna..." he murmured as the two of us came together, and the dark world around us blurred into something bright and full of stars, just for a moment.

His thighs were trembling as he leaned forward and kissed my neck, before he slowly withdrew from me. I almost expected him to just walk away, like I'd seen him do to so many others, but he gathered me in his arms, carrying me back toward the counters full of folded clothing at the center of the store.

"What are we going to do in the morning, Rhy?" I asked.

"Keep moving." He pressed a kiss to my temple. "Keep trying to find more moments where we aren't fucking miserable."

"I'm not miserable right now."

"Me either, sweetheart." He set me on the counter but kept me wrapped up in his arms. "You make me crazy. But I'm the closest I ever come to happy when you're around."

I smiled at the confession.

For a few minutes, that night, I believed that tomorrow would be even better. I believed even we really could be happy.

CHAPTER THIRTY-TWO

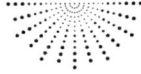

B*rianna*

A LOUD CRASH pulled me from sleep. For a second, I struggled to sit up, to remember where I was. Then I felt Rhyland curled behind me, still holding me, and it came rushing back. The transport. The escape. The warehouse.

Rhyland.

The psychic touch of Shade's mind tapped into mine as he checked in almost unconsciously, like someone whose first thought upon waking is to check the other side of the bed for their partner. I shook the odd thought away, trying to blink myself awake in the darkness.

"What the fuck was that?" he growled from the shelf above us.

"That would be a bomb," Rhyland said, ever the smartass. He tugged at me as if to pull me back, and though I'd have liked nothing more than to shut all this out and go back to sleep in his arms, I couldn't help feeling like whatever woke me wasn't the explosion.

Another one sounded somewhere close by, and the goods on the shelves rattled as they shook.

A loud bang, this one much closer, startled me into action.

"Someone's here," I said, scrambling off the shelf. The others leapt down to join me without a second's hesitation. Somehow, our unlikely group had become a team. Would have been nice to get to see what we could do together for more than a few hours, but if we'd been found by the angels, our time was up.

"Shit," Beckett muttered behind me. "We're caught."

"Time to kick some angel ass," Shade said gleefully, cracking his knuckles.

If we lived through this, I was going to have to ask if he *needed* to hurt people or if he just hated angels. Right now, I wasn't going to question my good luck that had somehow gotten him on my side.

"Grab whatever you can find to use for a weapon," I said, wishing I'd grabbed more than clothes and food in the evening. "Meet back here if there's time."

I took off at a run, crouched below the level of the shelves so when the angels made it in, they wouldn't see my head sticking up like a target. A second later, I heard the shatter of glass and saw a faint, golden glow that was probably supposed to make humans think calm and peaceful angels were here to fix all their problems.

I knew better.

"We know you're in here, demon," a voice called from near the entrance.

Damn it. Of course they weren't going to let Shade just waltz off into the sunset. He'd blown shit up to distract them. They probably wouldn't have cared much about a missing Nephilim. They'd just assume we'd die out here on our own, since they only knew one of us had escaped. But a demon? Especially one who stole an angel's Grace and tied him up? Yeah, probably not going to look the other way for that.

It wasn't Shade's fault though. He couldn't help what he was any more than we could help being expendable to the angels. Plus, the angel we'd tied up knew there were four of us, and he would have told the others. So they were out here hunting us all, not just Shade.

I strained my eyes to see anything I could in the store, anything that could be a weapon. We couldn't use flashlights now that the angels were here, but their glow gave us a bit of light to see by. Not enough to be a match for them, though. I remembered seeing some hunting tents over near the bicycles, so I crept that way as fast as I could without making more noise than I had to. I didn't know what kinds of weapons would be in a warehouse store, but they were better than nothing. They wouldn't hold the angels off for long, though. Not when they had things like Uriel's blade at their disposal.

I was almost there when the feathery, rippling sound of wings swept over me, sending a chill down my spine, and the warden landed in front of me.

"Well, hello, Brianna," he said with a twisted smile. "So, we meet again."

"Always a pleasure," I said, my eyes darting back and forth. I'd made it to the hardware section, which wasn't as good as hunting, but a hammer could do some damage, too.

He let out a low, menacing chuckle. "Oh, naïve little Nephilim, did you really think you'd survive in this abandoned store? How long were you planning to stay? Maybe you thought you'd live here?"

"Beats a maximum-security prison," I said, snatching a small hatchet off the rack beside me. The angel didn't even try to stop me. He looked amused.

I tightened my grip on the tool, preparing to throw it and run. I glanced over my shoulder, only to see one of the guards soaring over the shelves in our direction. Fuck.

I hurled the hatchet at the warden and dove for the opposite end of the shelves. I heard the hatchet hit what sounded like a pillow, and I knew the warden had fended it off with his wing. I hoped it had broken some bones at least, but I wasn't sticking around to find out. I shot past the end of the shelf and skidded to a stop as the guard dove in my direction. Suddenly, a ball of strange, black-tinged fire shot through the air like a comet and slammed into him. He screamed, his wings beating at the flames as they raced across his wingspan, devouring the feathers. He turned and dove for the source of the fire a few aisles over.

I raced that way, but when Shade saw me, he flung out an arm, gesturing wildly for me to go. "Run," he screamed just as the flaming angel slammed into him. They both went down, and I heard the thud of footsteps behind me. He was right. I was surrounded, and I didn't stand a chance without a weapon. I pivoted and ran for the hunting section at a dead sprint.

Darting around the corner, I found Beckett and Rhyland already there.

"You're okay?" Rhyland asked, not stopping what he was doing to check. He snatched boxes of ammunition while Beckett grabbed a hunting bow out of a case. I saw a glass case full of shotguns and ran to it. I didn't have time to find something to pad my hand, so I ripped my shirt over my head, wrapped it around my hand a couple times, and punched out the glass.

Shards rained down around me, and I felt the sharp edges tearing into the bare skin of my arm, leaving gashes in my flesh. Ignoring the pain, I yanked out a couple guns, tossing one to Rhyland. He tossed me a box of shells just as the warden touched down at the end of the aisle.

"You really think human weapons are a match for us?" he asked with a smug smile. "We've already taken down your demon, and he has more in his arsenal than a shotgun."

"No," I cried, fumbling as I loaded the next shell.

"Oh, yes," the warden said. "That was the hard part—taking out your protector. Three Nephilim are hardly enough of a challenge to break a sweat."

I glanced up to see that his wing was bleeding, the gold standing out against his pure white feathers. It was hard to look at something so awe-inspiring as an angel with his wings out. Even knowing he was evil, the sight still took my breath for a second. His huge wings were spread across the entire end of the aisle, the feathers gently rippling as they swayed lazily behind him.

But I knew the truth about angels. No matter how lovely to look at, they had used humanity as breeding mills to produce us—Nephilim. And they didn't even want the half-angel children they produced to love as their own or even to carry on their bloodline. They only created us to protect them from demons, to act as a living shield between them and their enemies on the battlefield. They were as cold and heartless as the demons themselves.

As if to reinforce my feelings about angels, I saw one of the guards heading for Shade where he lay injured. I knew he was still alive. When I reached for him with my mind, I could feel him still there, hanging on. I wasn't going to let that asshole kill him while he was down.

I turned away from the warden and ran. Beckett and Rhyland each stepped aside, letting me pass between them.

"I'm getting Shade," I said as I ran past them and darted out of the aisle. I heard a *twang!* sound a second later and knew Beckett must have fired the bow. I didn't turn back to see if he'd hit his mark. Racing for Shade, I almost missed the other guard changing course and swooping toward me. He soared over the shelves and dove at me. I dropped to my knees and slid under him, and he crashed into the shelf with a curse.

I scrambled to my feet and darted into the next aisle where Shade lay bound by glowing gold cuffs that swallowed his entire hands. I could smell his flesh burning where they touched his skin, but he only gritted his teeth, breathing hard.

"Shade," I cried, reaching for him. The guard leapt over the shelf at me, but I raised the shotgun and slammed it into his temple with all my might. He stumbled back, dropping to his knees.

"Get these fucking cuffs off me," Shade growled. "I can't fight without my hands."

Remembering the fire he threw that swallowed up the angel's wings, I shuddered. The warden was right—he was our protector, our most powerful ally.

"How do I get them off?" I asked, glancing back at the guard who had climbed back to his feet.

"The keys should be on him," Shade growled, glaring at the guard with such hatred it turned my blood cold.

Before I could move, the guard dove at us again.

"Get down," Shade yelled, throwing his shoulder into me to knock me off my feet. The guard slammed into him with such force that it would have thrown a Nephilim across the room. Shade only lowered his head to meet the angel, head-butting him in the face. They both stumbled back from the impact. Blood streamed from a wound on Shade's forehead where it had collided with the angel's. I leapt to my feet, leveling the gun at the angel and firing a blast.

He screamed and flew backwards into the shelf.

"Nice shot, angel-baby," Shade drawled like it was all a game, like blood wasn't pouring from his forehead into his eyes. He tossed his head, trying to get the wet hair off his forehead.

"Come on," I said, grabbing his arm.

A drop of blood dripped from his head onto my arm. I wouldn't have even noticed, but it burned like molten lava on my skin. I looked down to see that it had dripped into one of the cuts I'd gotten when I'd broken into the case to get the guns. I wiped my arm quickly on my pants, but the burning didn't cease. Instead, it grew, spreading up my arm like wildfire.

"Shade," I gritted out. If demon blood made someone feel like their body was on fire, a heads up would have been nice.

"What's wrong?" he asked, a frown creasing his brow as he saw the pain etched across my face. The fire had spread past my arm, my shoulder, and into the center of my chest. It raced down my limbs and pierced through my middle, settling at the back of my torso like someone was holding two burning irons to my skin. I tried to hold back the pain, to keep my head, but it overwhelmed me, and a scream tore from my throat.

"Brianna," Shade barked, grabbing for me. But I'd already fallen to my hands and knees. My black hair hung down in front of me, swaying sickeningly. I thought I was going to be sick as the pain became more intense, ripping at my flesh. I was vaguely aware of running footsteps, of Rhyland and Beckett calling my name. I couldn't answer. I clenched my teeth, holding back another scream as my body jerked as something thrust up against my skin from within, tearing the flesh on my back open.

For seconds, minutes, I lost awareness of everything but the pain gripping my body, the burning in my blood, the ripping and popping as bones snapped and something tore from my body. At last, the pain began to ebb, and I could feel an unwieldy weight on my back. Not only that, but it seemed to be part of me, as I found myself moving the new limbs as if they were my own.

I pushed myself slowly to my feet, trying to catch my breath, and nearly lost my balance at the weight on my back. While I'd been down, I seemed to have attracted the attention of everyone in the place. The warden and the two injured guards stood gaping. Beckett and Rhyland stared at me as if they couldn't comprehend what they were seeing. Shade sank to his knees, gazing at me with nothing short of reverence.

I glanced back over my shoulder, trying to understand the new sensation on my back, as if new limbs had thrust themselves out of my back from within, growing to full size in minutes.

But they weren't limbs.

Behind me stretched a pair of glorious, black-feathered wings.

CHAPTER THIRTY-THREE

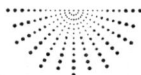

B *rianna*

"WHAT IS SHE?" breathed one of the angels, his face stricken with horror. "W-what is that creature?"

"Dead," the warden ground out.

At the same moment, Shade spoke. "My queen."

I tried to move to one side the warden dove at me, his friend following. But the sudden appearance of the wings made me lurch clumsily. In my panic, I tried to leap aside, but my wings caught my balance, and I soared into the air. I heard the frantic beating of my wings behind me. The wind they caused blew back Shade's hair as he jumped to his feet and ran toward me while Rhyland and Beckett struggled to reach me, too.

Suddenly, I lost control of my new wings and plunged to the ground. My knees buckled on impact. The angels were waiting. One of them drove a blade into my side, a pain so bright and blazing that my back arched as I screamed. The other one was already behind me, catching my chin and drawing his blade across my throat. I barely understood what happened, but I suddenly couldn't speak, couldn't scream. My throat and chest were wet and when my fingers touched my skin, and I realized he'd sliced my throat open.

I heard an anguished roar as if from far away, but the echo inside my head let me know it was Shade. Everyone around me was covered in blood. Rhyland looked horrified through the blood splattered across his face. Beckett was a blur, moving with his weapons to attack the angel who had just slit my throat.

I crumpled to the ground, desperate to help my men as they fought for their lives.

But I couldn't breathe, couldn't move. I was dying.

Blackness swallowed me.

My body flushed with heat, heat that consumed me, that burned until I screamed. I could scream again. Fuck. My vision cleared. I stared down at my blood-soaked clothes. Then I struggled to my feet, my slick fingers touching my throat. It was *healed.*

As the pain faded, energy and fury washed through me in its stead.

Thew room was in chaos around me. Angels had seized Rhyland and Beckett, and two of them had Shade. They had his arms in chains, but they were about to cut his throat.

"She can't be killed," one of the angels said, his voice cut through with fear.

The warden turned to see me, and his eyes widened. In their reflection, I could see how eerie I looked with my black wings spread to either side, my hair waving around my face and what looked like flames crackling around my body.

"I'm sure there's a way," the warden gritted.

"There isn't." Noah's voice resounded through the room. I turned to see him standing at the end of an aisle, his eyes wide as he stared at me with a mixture of stunned awe and resignation. "If she is what I think she is, you can't kill her," he said quietly, his eyes rounded as he still stared at me like... Well, like I'd grown a pair of fucking wings.

"What am I?" I demanded.

"You need to get her out of sight before the demons learn she exists," Noah said, striding forward.

Shade, despite his struggle with his guards, turned that worshipful expression on me again, and I wondered what the hell was going on. "You're *her*," he said, his awe-struck voice so different from the lazy drawl he usually used.

"When they come for her," Noah warned, "nothing will stop them. They'll die for her."

I really wanted to know what the hell I was, but one look at Shade's face let me know that Noah was right. Shade looked like he'd just laid eyes on god himself.

No time to figure it out now, though. I needed to get myself and my men the fuck out. If I had wings, maybe I had other powers, too. Once we escaped, I'd worry about if I was a monster or not.

I tried to imagine flames like Shade had produced, imagining them blossoming at my fingers. My body flushed with heat, but nothing happened.

"Get her," the warden told his angels, but no one moved. *They* hadn't realized yet that I didn't have those demon powers like Shade. None of them moved, as if they were scared to touch me.

"There's a better way to deal with this," Noah promised. "You know you can't kill her, but you can kill *them*. And she wouldn't want you to do that."

There was a mocking, cruel edge in his voice—and I could have sworn, a tinge of jealousy. The warden's mouth curved into an equally cruel smile as he held a blade to Beckett's throat.

"Let me have them," Noah said, holding up a hand. "Let me have all of them. I can keep her under control as long as they're alive."

"Under control?" I turned to Noah with a laugh. "I don't think so."

"Okay," the warden agreed suddenly. "Fine. Just... get her under control."

"Put on the cuffs, Brianna," Noah told me, tossing them to me. He didn't even move toward me, and the cuffs clattered to the floor. They were really scared of what I could do. Even Noah. I could see it in his eyes. Fear and... Betrayal. Fury. "Then we'll go on home."

"No," Shade said. "Brianna, you can get out of here. You can save yourself. You can fly home, to your true home, where you belong—"

One of the guards slammed his boot into Shade's ribs so hard I could hear them snap. Shade doubled over. I tensed to spring at them, but Noah held up a hand.

"You know what they're going to do to him," Noah said, his voice a cajoling taunt. The room had gone very quiet. "Pick up the cuffs, Brianna."

I glanced around the room, barely seeing the beautiful angels now with their wings that filled this dark space. All I could focus on was Shade, obviously in pain but climbing to his feet again, and Rhyland and Beckett, struggling against the guards. They were eager to get to me, to help me, despite the confusion written across their faces. They would protect me. I had to do the same for them.

I knelt and picked up the cuffs.

"Good choice," Noah said.

The second I snapped them closed, the power and energy that had flooded my veins seemed to ebb.

I crumpled toward the ground, but Noah snatched me, scooping me up against his chest. I tried to push away from him, hating the poisonous cuffs that sapped my strength, hating for him to be anywhere near me.

I couldn't escape him, though. He carried me toward the front of the building, where his transport waited. They must have called in reinforcements to track us down.

"I need them alive," he called over his shoulder. "All of them."

Behind me, I heard the sounds of the guards dragging my men out.

We emerged into the sunshine, and there was a truck waiting in front of us, to take us back to prison… If we were lucky.

"Where are you taking me?" I asked Noah, but the burning sensation was back as my new magic tore to escape the bonds he'd put on me. I let out a moan of pain.

The last thing I saw was Noah's smug face staring down at me before the world faded black.

Thank you for reading! What's up with Brianna's black wings? Where is Noah taking them? Click here to find out in the explosive second book in the trilogy: http://books2read.com/angelsofchaos2

To GET UPDATES, insider info, and other exciting exclusives, please join our newsletters!

May's: https://mailchi.mp/maydawson/signup

Alexa's: https://www.subscribepage.com/angelsofchaos

Printed in Great Britain
by Amazon